The Red Bonnet

By Patrick Blosse

DiaBlo Publishing

First edition

Printed by Kindle Direct Publishing in the United Kingdom

ISBN: 9798612835493

Disclaimer

This is a work of fiction. All names, characters, businesses, places, events, locales, and incidents are either the products of the author's imagination or used in a fictitious manner. Any resemblance to actual persons, living or dead, or actual events is purely coincidental.

24th December 1967

It was one of those crisp, winter days, when the sun tilts in low and bright with a cold, bloodless light. I had settled on a brisk walk into town to stretch my legs and clear a few cobwebs, resulting in the purchase of a small jar of very strong, instant coffee and a determination to accompany it with a large Danish pastry or something stuffed with cream.

The baker's heaved gently with like-minded shoppers. It was an old-fashioned shop, with a tall wooden rack selling yesterday's sausage rolls and pasties at half-price. I queued dutifully. Three large women picked over the pallid remains, comparing their finds and their common ailments with so little pause for breath that it was impossible to tell what was going soggy and what might have strange spots on it. I stood behind two small children discussing, with the intensity that only 6-year olds can achieve, the relative merits of macaroons and those things that look like ice-cream cornets but are really made of marshmallow.

But my eye was caught by an older woman in a bright red bonnet who was already being served. The bonnet stood out like a beacon. I was drawn to it. Not just because it was intensely red; it was out of place, much too '19th century' to be worn in today's modern world. Two strands of bright red material hung at its sides, ready to be knotted against the onslaught of any wind and weather that wanted to wrestle it from the elderly lady's head. She was ordering a spelt and honey loaf and giving detailed instructions about how it should be sliced; half thick and half thin, some for sandwiches and some for toasting. I toyed with the mathematics of how far down the loaf it should be sliced thinly in order to get exactly the same number of thick and thin slices when the old lady turned her head and nodded to me with a knowing smile. I had a fleeting, uncomfortable feeling that she knew what I was thinking. Or was she simply sharing a common appreciation of the macaroon v. cornet debate that raged between us?

My attention was diverted by an assistant asking what I wanted, and I realised that I hadn't yet tackled the knotty choice between cinnamon swirl and Viennese whirl. Before my brain had engaged, the old woman was nudging past me with a brown paper bag tucked firmly under her arm. What made me follow her, I shall never know, but I made a brief and incoherent apology and tried to sweep out after her. Three fat ladies barred my path like the many-handed beasts at the gates of Tartarus. By the time I had wriggled past them, the red bonnet was nowhere to be seen.

At least, that is, until a tall gentleman, balancing on a walking cane, tottered away and there she was, her nose pressed close to a shop window 50 yards up the hill. She turned towards me the moment she came into view and shared her enigmatic smile again. Had she known I would follow her? I tried to look unconcerned but not unfriendly. I fear that the result was frighteningly wide of the mark. She moved off again, heading up the High Street, bonnet first, moving at a pace that belied her age. I followed. There is no rational reason why I should do such a thing. I am not a stalker by nature. I am not nosey. I usually treat other people's affairs with sublime indifference tempered by a touch of respect and plain good manners. But this lady and her strange bonnet and knowing smile had captured my interest. I followed at a respectful distance. Exactly what that is in feet and inches, I couldn't tell you. It makes little difference. The old lady was moving so fast, I was pressed to stay close enough to see where she went.

She must have known. After a hundred yards or so, she paused at the entrance to a narrow alleyway. I am positive now that it was a deliberate ploy to make sure I didn't lose sight of her. By the time I reached the alley she had disappeared from view again, but it was clear that I was meant to follow. Three shallow, worn steps led up from the High Street between two old buildings that were crowding together for warmth. There was no more than the width of a door between them. The path led upwards and turned quite sharply to the left after only a few paces so that the noise and bustle of the High Street was quickly muffled. Soon I could hear nothing but my own echoing footsteps and the drip of an overflowing gutter. I have lived here for 50 years, but I could not recall ever seeing this passageway before. The path continued to rise and soon I had emerged above the rooftops of the High Street and was looking down at a town that was now partly hidden in mist.

There she was again. This time, only two doors away, along a terrace of ancient cottages that looked out over the town and the hills beyond. And this time there was no doubt. She stepped inside the open door of the cottage, beckoning me to follow. I was wary, but as I think back now, I was not fearful. I could hear jollity and music. I could hear children laughing. There was some sort of party going on inside the house, and I had just been given an invitation to join it. I stepped across the threshold.

27th December 2017

"Dad, when did Grandad disappear?"

"I don't know. Late 60s – something like that."

"Can't you remember what year? What time of year it was?"

"Christmas Eve."

"I thought so. It was his birthday, wasn't It? How old were you then?"

"Two or three – something like that. I never knew him really. I'd have to find a picture of him to even remember what he looked like. Why the sudden interest?"

"There's something on Facebook – look. You ought to see it. They've found a body – up on the old hospital site - where they're building that new estate."

"So?"

"It could be him."

"What makes you think that? It's hardly likely is It? He's been gone for nearly 50 years."

"Not 'nearly 50 years', Dad. I reckon it's exactly 50 years. He disappeared on his 50th birthday, right? On Christmas Eve - when you were two years old."

"Or three."

"You must have been two, because that would make it 1967. He was found - get this - on Christmas Eve – three days ago. That means he disappeared on his 50th birthday and they found him on his 100th!"

"Come on, son, that's stretching it. You're just making the facts fit your over-active imagination."

"Ah, but, listen, 'Among the bones and few scraps of clothing that remained was found an unopened jar of Marks and Spencer's Special Colombian Blend coffee which bore a sell-by date of June 1968, indicating that the unknown corpse might have lain there for about 50 years.' I rest my case."

"He did go out looking for coffee. Your Grandmother never forgot that. Never drank coffee again 'til the day she died. But it's just a coincidence."

27th December 1917

I stepped over the threshold. The front door led straight into a cramped living room. Half a dozen or so assorted bodies packed it untidily, vying for space with a small Christmas tree and some haphazardly thrown decorations, clumps of holly and mistletoe. A log fire burnt in a small grate, roasting them slowly, but they were too busy to notice. A small, pink-faced, middle-aged lady thumped an upright piano, trying her best to keep up with a tall, spindly gentleman who was making mincemeat of an old music hall song. He wore a finely decorated waistcoat with a watch chain that stretched alarmingly when he aimed for the high notes. Sadly, his aim was poor, but his efforts were not unrewarded. Either the entertainment, or the bubbly concoction in the glasses they were all holding, had filled the room with a bonhomie that was infectious, and he was being cheered and jeered in equal measure.

I searched for a red bonnet, but it was not in the room. My eyes came to rest on a woman sitting in a well-stuffed armchair near the fire. In her arms was a tiny baby, gurgling in time to the music. But it was the face of the woman herself that brought me up short. It was my mother. Not the mother that I visit in a nursing home with her face like parchment and her liver-spotted hands. Not the mother with Alzheimer's and angina and a vicious tongue. This was a vibrant young woman, full of life and ambition; a woman with a wide smile and bright eyes. The mother that I kept in my wallet.

The spindly fellow brought his rendition to a close, to a polite round of relief. He grabbed a full glass from the top of the piano and proposed a toast; heart-felt words that were stilted but genuine. He welcomed his first grandson into the family, heaped praises on the baby's mother and wished the parents a long and happy union with many more little-ones to follow. A comment which caused the pink lady at the piano to turn bright pink and the rest of the company to titter with embarrassment. It was not until he proposed a second toast to absent warriors and "God speed for a safe return" that there was a palpable change in mood. But good cheer soon returned. 'Old Spindly' offered his rendition of 'Burlington Bertie From Bow', but it was gently turned down on the grounds that they didn't want to curdle the baby's milk, and the party settled into polite conversation. None of it was directed at me.

I was trying to make sense of what was happening when a knock at the door brought conversation to a halt. The door was opened to reveal a small boy of perhaps 12 or 13 in an ill-fitting uniform. An older boy's peaked cap wobbled on his head. His trousers too must have been built for an altogether more robust individual. They only touched where they were gripped by his bicycle clips and tightly-pulled leather belt. He held out a small, buff envelope and asked if he was to wait. There was a world of difference between the quiet of a room where everyone had stopped talking and the deathly emptiness that filled that space as the telegram was reverently passed from hand to hand.

My mother put the baby down in its cot by the fire, took the envelope and held it in shaky hands. The tall, thin man knelt and covered both her hands and the envelope with his long, bony fingers, but she gently pulled them free, resolved to read the message herself.

There was a tap on my shoulder. I turned to see the red-bonneted woman standing there, beckoning me to follow her again, but I was rooted to the spot. She tugged my elbow, eager that we should leave. I had no choice. My feet were guided by her, not by me. I found myself outside the cottage, the red-bonnet bobbing away down the hill before me. Beyond her I could see the church spire and a few chimney pots peeking out above the mist; behind me, my mother's muffled sobs declared the contents of the envelope. I shared her tears. Memories of a childhood spent longing for a father, like most of the other boys at school, tumbled through me as I hurried after the receding figure of the strange woman and her beacon-like hat.

I had almost caught up with her as the path narrowed, squeezing its way between the two over-friendly buildings. She turned the tight bend just ahead of me but by the time I had covered the ground between us and almost tripped down the three shallow steps that led into the High Street, she had disappeared again.

27th December 2017

"He was a navy man, wasn't he?"

"Who?"

"Grandad – in the war – he was in the navy, wasn't he?

"Oh, we're back on him again, are we?"

"Well?"

"What?"

"Was he in the navy?"

"Yes. What's that got to do with anything?"

"I'm interested, that's all. Trying to get a handle on the man. Piece his life together, you know."

"No, I don't know. Why should you want to know so much about him when I don't give a - don't give tuppence? He was my father, but he pissed off when I was just a toddler and left my mother to bring me up all on her own. She went through hell for 20 years trying to start a family before I turned up. She spent 16 years as a one-parent family, and then she retired lonely and broke and then she died. I owe him nothing. We owe him nothing."

"Sorry, Dad. Didn't realise. It's just - he's my Grandad, and I wanted to know a bit about him. I didn't mean to hurt you."

"You're on about this damn body again, aren't you?"

"They've given out a few more details. They think he was a sailor."

"What? Someone took a lick of one of his bones and thought they tasted salty?"

"Not quite. There were a few bits and pieces that hadn't disintegrated, and one of them was an old, navy-issue clasp knife."

"Oh well, that clinches it. Hundreds of thousands of demobbed sailors after the war, but I'm sure Grandad was the only one who took a knife home."

"What was his war wound?"

"Now what?

"You told me once he limped. Something that happened in the war."

"Ha! War wound, I like that."

"I thought you said once – "

"Mum used to love this story. He was a gunner on a cruiser out in the far east. Shelling raids on Japanese oil refineries and the like. Well, they're laid up in Trincomalee; not even actually operational or anything, just practicing, and he only went and dropped a bloody shell on his foot, didn't he? She laughed like a drain every time she told it."

"Well, I'm glad that cheered you up. Listen to this, '...further inspection of the remains shows that the unknown male suffered trauma to the left foot at some time with a number of bones having been broken. This might have been a sports injury or could have been sustained in a traffic accident. A few objects were also found with the body, including a Royal Navy clasp knife of the type widely issued in the 1940s and 50s, a pocket watch, some coins, an unopened jar of coffee and a few strips of clothing, including a brown leather belt and one, size 7, black leather shoe. Police are interested to hear from anyone who thinks they might be able to identify the victim.'"

"He's a victim now, is he?"

"That's what it says here."

27th June 1942

She had disappeared again. I looked up and down the street, but there was no red bonnet in sight. I turned around in the vain hope that I had somehow overtaken her, but no, there was no sign. There was no sign of the alleyway either. Only seconds ago I had stumbled down the worn steps that led up from the High Street to the narrow passageway. Now – no steps, no alley, no old buildings leaning in. Instead, I stared at the glass-fronted entrance to Timothy Whites. And staring back at me, reflected in its wide, glass doors - me. Me in my number one dress uniform - my blues - regulation wear when ashore.

Nothing was right anymore. Nothing was making any sense. I stood there, staring at my reflection, trying to remember how that thin, strong, tanned young body had turned into the overweight, unattractive, uncared-for one that I carted around today. Today? What was today? It sure as hell wasn't Christmas Eve anymore. No Christmas lights strung from the lampposts. No slanting winter sunshine and breath freezing on the air. The sun was high in the sky and people were strolling past in summer dresses and shirt sleeves. I closed my eyes, hoping that this ridiculous dream would end; that I could wake up and find myself at home, with my feet up, enjoying my coffee and my Danish pastry.

The town hall clock struck, and that's when I knew exactly what day this was. June, or was it July 1942 – I was on a 48-hour pass from Portsmouth. We'd both wangled 48-hour passes for the same weekend, and we intended to make the most of them. I remembered I'd called in to Timothy Whites on my way to meet her. They had a chemist's and I needed some essential supplies if our weekend was going to be the success I hoped for. The clock struck a second time and I spurred into action. If I was to relive my life, this was as good a day to start from as any I could recall. It was nearly a 100-yards to the Town Hall, and even though it was uphill, I was screeching to a halt under the clock before the twelfth chime had faded away.

There she was, already waiting, my little jenny wren. The sight of a uniformed whirlwind kicking up sparks on the stone setts of the High Street gave her plenty of warning of my arrival. She smiled that beautiful, angelic, sexy, superior smile that said she was not only pleased to see me but also that she was highly surprised to see me arrive on time.

"Are you in a hurry?" she asked. I told her I didn't want to waste a minute of the time we had together, but I meant it so much more sincerely this time She was so beautiful, so young, so full of hope and, this time, I *knew* she was going to be my wife. We had already agreed, in the brief exchange of letters since we first met, that we would go to the pictures and then get tea at the Tudor Rose Tea Rooms. No coupons would be spared. We had a choice of *Mrs Miniver* at the Odeon, or *Yankee Doodle Dandy* at the Bughouse. It was no contest. My jenny wren wasn't going to be seen dead in The Plaza, no matter what they were showing. And didn't I know why the place was called the Bughouse? So, I was going to see *Mrs Miniver* again. I couldn't remember much about it from the first time and I was hoping we might be too busy in the dark picture house to be bothered by it this time round. The next 2 hours dissolved into a joyful haze. A leisurely walk took us to the top of the town. There was a florist on the corner, just before the cinema. I plucked a flower head from the pavement display and stuck it in her cap tally. The florist was none too pleased at first, but she could see we were a couple of lovers in love, and sporting the King's uniform at that, so she waved us off – I knew she would. I expect we got the same two seats. It felt the same. I relaxed into my new-found freedom. It was too dark to see a red bonnet in here. Maybe I'd never see her again. The film came and went. We held hands, we hardly talked, we kissed; we shared popcorn and a coke with two straws. When we came out, the sun was brighter than ever. We stepped into it, arm in arm, blind to everything but our own happiness. She kissed me lightly on the cheek, freed herself and said she needed to 'freshen up'. She gave me her best '19 and never been kissed' face and skipped back up the steps into the cinema to seek out the ladies' rest room.

I pulled a packet of Woodbines from my pocket and chose the least crumpled one, but before I could set fire to it, a battered old taxi pulled up to the curb in front of me. An even older but surprisingly nimble cab driver leapt out to open the back door, and indicated that I was meant to get in. I'd started to explain that I hadn't ordered a taxi and he must be there for someone else when I saw a movement inside the cab. It was her. She leaned forward from her seat in the far corner. The sun, slanting through the cab's window, bounced off her bonnet making it look brighter and redder than ever. She held out her hand and I knew with crushing certainty that I wouldn't be taking my gorgeous jenny

17

wren to the Tea House any time soon. Before I knew it, I was inside the cab and the driver was shutting the door behind me. It sounded like a cell door slamming. I stared out at the cinema steps, hoping for one last glimpse of her, but the ancient cab spat out black smoke, executed a U-turn and trundled back down the High Street.

3rd January 2018

"So, what are you going to do, Dad?"

"I thought I might pop up the allotment for an hour or two. Want to come?"

"What are you going to do - about Grandad?"

"Nothing."

"But they want people to come forward. We could help th...."

"We could stay out of it and lead our lives in peace."

"But – "

"We have no proof it's him."

"But the knife, the coffee, the foot – "

"We don't have any proof. You're just guessing – hoping more like. A million sailors came home from the war with navy issue knives. We don't even know if one of them was Grandad. People buy coffee every day. Have you any idea how many people in this town alone could have a broken bone in their foot – for any one of a hundred reasons? Did they find a wallet with his name in it? A letter with his address? A photograph? An ID tag? No. They would have said. There is no reason why your Grandfather would be found on a derelict building site."

"But statistically – "

"What do you mean 'statistically'? Statistics don't come into it."

"But – yeah, any one thing might not be significant but when you multiply them together – it's the law of probability."

"Probability bollocks. Don't give me all that statistical bullshit. The only statistics I believe is 'lies, damn lies and statistics'. You can prove anything you like if you chuck enough numbers at it."

"I think you're wrong."

"I know what I'm talking about. That bastard had an affair with another woman, buggered off and never came back. That's all I know about him and that's all I want to know!"

18th May 1947

We passed the florist's and the Town Hall, stopped outside Timothy Whites to let a young woman with a pram cross the road, carried on down the hill, past the baker's and over the old bridge, round the back of the bus station and then up the other side of the river. Now I knew where were headed. If there was one place in this town that I knew better than anywhere, it was this great, sprawling mess of a building ahead of us; the old hospital. Closed now, but I knew its corridors like the back of my hand. Fear gripped me. What horrors did they have in store for me now? I reached for the taxi's door handle with the vague idea that I could jump out – get away. But I was powerless. There was no strength in me – not in my hands or in my heart. The woman in the red bonnet covered my hand with hers but I felt no comfort.

The hospital gates were not barred and padlocked, as I expected. An ambulance pulled in ahead of us, its bells jangling, and took the slip road to the emergency ward. We parked right outside the main reception, in the middle of the brightly painted 'No Parking' zone, but it didn't seem to matter. I stepped out of the cab and she stepped out on her side and made straight for the entrance. I followed her up the steps and into the main building. The smell of the hospital brought so many memories flooding back. I knew where we were going. Maternity was two floors up and three long corridors away. There were lifts but visitors weren't encouraged to use them. We followed my well-worn path. It felt, as ever, like a condemned man's final walk to the scaffold.

3rd January 2018

"You never said anything before about him having an affair. Grandma never said anything."

"Well, that's what your Grandma always thought. She wouldn't have talked to you about it, would she? A disgrace like that. She kept herself to herself, but it ate her up in the end."

"She was certainly a grumpy old cow."

"That's enough of that! Don't talk about things you know nothing about – and don't ever talk about your Grandmother like that again."

"Sorry."

"You're 17 – nearly an adult – and you know nothing. Kids today - you live a life of luxury. Everything done for you. Roof over your head, all the food you can eat. Every medical aid you can think of. You have no idea what it was like for your Grandmother, growing up through the depression, living through the war, poor as a church mouse for all those years, losing all them babies..."

"What babies?"

18th May 1947

Bare corridors of dead-eyed patients. Nurses locked in their own worlds of bedpans and buzzers, bustling from room to room like eager bees. And me, locked in my own thoughts.

I noticed I was limping quite badly, like I used to years ago. "Where are we?" I called out to the woman in the red bonnet. I meant 'when' are we, but she knew that. There was no reply. She just beckoned me to keep following – as though I had any choice. Is this what dreams are? Memories strung together for no apparent reason? And yet, it was clear that I was being led – a guided tour of my past life with no commentary. And who was the guide, me or the silent old lady in her bright red hat? Was I in control, or just an observer - an unwilling follower?

I realised that I was no longer in uniform. When that change had happened, I could not recall. But then, I wouldn't have been in uniform if I was coming here. The war was over by the time the babies started coming. Fuck! I was in my demob suit. That could mean only one thing. 1947, we were both demobilised in the Autumn of '46, married in the December, and the twins came in the May of '47. Yeah, I know, you do the maths, but neither of us wanted to tie the knot 'til the war was over, and we were both home safe and sound.

We reached the maternity ward, passing on our left the glass fronted baby store, where rows of new-borns were filed for safe keeping until they were needed.

There was no need to look in there. The main ward was like any other. A dozen beds neatly stacked along each of the two long walls, expectant mothers to the left and new mothers to the right. No ante-natal and pre-natal rubbish in those days. You could be in your bed, waiting for your baby to be born, staring across the ward at a woman who'd just delivered a small elephant and couldn't wait to tell you all about it in every gory detail. The place stank of disinfectant, barely masking the lingering odours of the workhouse that this building had been until war broke out.

I closed my eyes, not wanting to know which side of the ward we were visiting.

I heard her call my name. There she was, three beds in, on the left. She looked pale but she was sitting up, smiling and waving, eager and happy to see me. I leant down to kiss her. She smiled. I wiped a tear from my eye.

"You alright. Did you get it?"

"What?" I said, searching my pockets. I wondered what it was I meant to have brought.

"Don't be so silly. Did you get the job?" She misinterpreted my hesitation and reached out her hand. "Don't worry, darling. There'll be other jobs. We'll be fine."

It clicked. "I was just teasing you. Of course, I got the job. Start next Monday." She sank back into the bed, the relief instantly giving her body permission to relax.

"We're going to be so fine," she said, but I knew we weren't. God, how I wished the world would swallow me up, suck me back to my home, back to where I didn't know what the future holds. Where was the old woman, with her bright red bonnet and her annoying smile when you really wanted her?

"You OK?"

"I feel a bit faint."

"Should be me saying that," she said. "Sit down on the bed. Nobody'll mind."

"I'll get a chair," I said, stood up, and fainted to the floor.

3rd January 2018

"Well, if you won't call the police, I will."

"No, you won't."

"Why not?"

"Because I don't want you to."

"Because you hate him for leaving you and Grandma? This might prove that he didn't abandon you – that he couldn't come home because he'd had some sort of accident. Wouldn't that solve everything?"

"Of course it wouldn't. Knowing what happened isn't going to change anything, is it? It won't bring him back and it won't give your Grandmother back any of those lost years. I'd just have to bear the knowledge that she wasted all that time hating him, when she could have been mourning him and living off the good memories. How's that going to make me feel? I want things to stay the way they are."

14th July 1957

When I came round, I was in the waiting room, outside the delivery suite. I knew these walls so well. I had sat here, smoking and fretting, for more hours than I cared to remember. I'd paced this floor off and on for over 20 years, and in all that time, the paint and the curtains, the carpet and the view from the window had never changed.

Those twins, those poor little half-formed twins that were born in 1947. Jean and Joan, we called them. They wouldn't let us christen them, but we gave them a decent burial. They were just the start. Was it 2 of 3 miscarriages before Derek came along – six weeks early? He counted as a success when he lived for all of 2 weeks. He was so tiny, so delicate. He lived in his little incubator, fed through pipes, his oxygen pumped from a great metal tube, humidity and temperature controlled by nurses every minute of the day like gardeners tending their marrow. But there was going to be no prize for Derek. Just a plot next to Jean and Joan. We never even got to hold him before he passed. We gave up for a while then. It was all too much. It was 5 years before we tried again. The doctors didn't like the idea, but it wasn't their lives that were empty. My little jenny wren, so strong and full of life when we were courting, had the life-blood sucked out of her in those years, but she was a fighter, and so desperate for a family. We both were. They told us about the risks. She was over 30 now, and that's no great age, but with her history they said they couldn't advise us to try for another one. That didn't sound like a firm enough 'no' to either of us, so we went ahead anyway.

Philip was born in 1957. Before he was born, she spent most of the time in bed, and if she wasn't there, she was up here at the hospital having check-ups. He went almost full-term. We couldn't have been happier. We were going to have a bonny, bouncing baby.

The birth was just a mess. God knows what happened. Breach, they said, his cord was wrapped around his neck; a forceps delivery. The list was too long. It was all a confusing, noisy mess. I sat in this room and listened to the screams. I couldn't make them stop. I can hear them now, echoing through the walls...

He was a floppy baby. They said he was just tired because the birth had been "a bit traumatic". My arse. We took him home 2 weeks later, but we knew even then that something wasn't right. Cerebral palsy they said in the end, but it took them 4 years to say it. The Spastics Society helped us out. They said it was the hospital's fault, but how were we going to prove that, with our history? Did we sleep much all those years? I suppose we must have done but God knows when. He never spoke. He never learnt to feed himself. He was never out of nappies. It was pneumonia took him in the end, just a week before his 5th birthday. And, God help me, it was a blessed relief.

How long did I sit there, my head in my hands, trying not to listen to the echoing screams bouncing round my head? Seconds? Hours? I'll never know. I heard the door creak open. What fresh horror was this? Would the woman in the red bonnet lead in a procession of dead babies? I couldn't bear to look up.

3rd January 2018

"What babies?"

"I thought we'd dropped this subject."

"You did – I didn't."

"You get this attitude from your mother, don't you? I never raised you to question your father like this."

"You raised me to think for myself, didn't you? You should be proud."

"Arrogant little prig. If it was up to me, I'd send you back."

"I love you too, Dad. What babies?"

"OK. I'll tell you – and then we'll drop the subject."

17th October 1962

There was another creak, like a heavy, oak door on ancient hinges.

"Can I help you?" It was the vicar from St. Francis. Not the one we have now. The old one, the famous one who'd done *The Epilogue* on the BBC.

We weren't in the hospital waiting room anymore. It had dissolved into the church. My plastic chair was now a wooden pew. My hands no longer covered my eyes. They were clasped in prayer. The bitter draft that always swept through these pews now plucked at my trouser legs and a shiver rippled through my body.

"Are you alright? I'm always happy to talk if you want to." He smiled at me benevolently as though a simple touch from him could solve all my ills.

It was right after Philip died that we took to religion. We were never non-believers, but we'd never been that devout, if you know what I mean. We went to church for Harvest Festival and maybe a Christmas Carol Concert or two, but that was about it. But somehow, when Philip was gone, there was a void that had to be filled for us both and we found it at St. Francis'. She suggested we even joined the choir and we were welcomed with open arms. They said she was a lovely contralto, and they'd be really pleased if I'd come along too and help with making the tea! They can be very hurtful sometimes, these Christians.

"I'll just leave you to your thoughts."

"No!" I couldn't bear that. I asked him to sit with me, but we couldn't talk. He was good at listening but that's a redundant skill when your partner has no conversation. We sat in silence for some minutes. Perhaps he was frustrated that I would not tell him why I was there, but he gave nothing away. Patiently, he waited but I did not feel the need to share. Eventually, he tried small talk. He asked about my good lady wife. I told him she was all those things. He could remember her name but not mine, it seemed. I didn't mind. I couldn't remember his. Trevor? Tremayne? No, that was some character in a book I was reading. My mind was drifting. He got up, apologising that he had parochial business to see to.

"Stay as long as you like," he said. "Daphne will be along in a minute, but she won't bother you." So that was why I had been sent here. "She comes in every Wednesday with my clean vestments. She does a quick tidy round in the vestry and moves some of the dust about in here. Just ignore her."

I had never ignored Daphne. Who could? It just hadn't occurred to me before that this was why I was here. Daphne. Rita Hayworth with Veronica Lake's hair and Betty Grable's legs. When she smiled, the sun sat up and took notice. The vicar left, creaking the door behind him, and like a scene from a French farce, the vestry door opened and in she swept. That was our standing joke. My first view of her was her swaying backside as she reversed through the vestry door, waving her broom from side to side and kicking up dust. This was the day we'd met. Was that only 5 years ago? It seemed so much more. I could have got up and crept out right then. It would have been the right thing to do. But no.

The lassitude that had followed me this far was not about to lose its grip. I must have sat and watched her for 3 or 4 minutes, collecting up hymn books, straightening kneelers, dusting shelves and window-sills, before she spotted me at the back of the church. She let out a tiny scream, but I tried not to take offence. I reassured her that, despite appearances, I wasn't a rapist or a mad, ecumenical axe-murderer. Clearly, there were less people seeking sanctuary in churches these days. She had been cleaning here for 3 years and had never found a lost soul in the back pews before.

"Are you alright?" she asked. "I'm always happy to listen if you'd like." Isn't that what the vicar had said? Somehow, it sounded more sincere coming from her, as though her smile really could solve all my ills.

Why did I open up to her the way I did? Was it because I thought I knew her then the way I know her now? Was this our first meeting or a re-run? I could not tell. I did not care. It was good to be in her company again. We talked. Partly of this and that, mainly about me. In that first talk, she learnt more about my life, my highs and lows, my joys and sorrows, than I had ever shared with anyone – even with my little jenny wren.

And so, we met there every week. I always worked a short shift on Wednesdays, so it was easy to pop in on the way home. Ten minutes with Daphne was enough to see me through the rest of the week. I think she looked forward to it too. We enjoyed each other's company, that's all, and the peace and quiet of the church, away from the stench and noise of traffic and the bother of other people. We exchanged snippets of mundane news or just sat in peace together, grateful for someone to share our solitude with. We never kissed. We didn't do anything that anyone but the prudest prude could tut at, and yet, guilt accompanied our every meeting.

At home, our lives picked up from that point on. It was the early 1960s. There was a smell of change in the air. Teenagers were taking over the world, blowing away the dust and detritus of the post-war years. We were too old to be a part of it, but we could see it happening. I was made up to Supervisor so there was a little more money coming in. In a year or two we'd shed some of the weight of losing Philip. We were starting to settle to the idea of a childless future, as the fates had always decreed...

Daphne jumped up, suddenly concerned that she'd spent too long with me. She gathered up her broom and dusters with a cheery "see you again maybe" and disappeared into the vestry.

There was a creak behind me. I turned slowly, expecting to see the vicar returning, but no, it was her. I should have known. Her bonnet shone as bright as ever. She came over to where I sat and eased herself in beside me. She took my hand in hers and my eyes felt heavy. I must have fallen into a deep slumber.

3rd January 2018

"That's such a sad story."

"Except it's not a story is it. That was their life. They fell in love. They wanted a big family, but it wasn't to be. Then I came along and just when they thought they'd put all their problems behind them, your Grandad finds some other woman and leaves us in the lurch. Yes, it's sad, but we've managed without him all these years. I can't see the point of digging it up all over again."

"Not your best metaphor, Dad, in the circumstances."

"Maybe not."

"So, who was this other woman? Did she get interviewed by the police?"

"Nobody knew who she was, and there was no body, don't forget. No-one thought he was dead. It's not a crime to leave your family and go off and live with someone else. It never has been. As far as anyone knew, no crime was committed, so why would the police want to interview anyone?"

"So, nobody knew her name."

"I think Mum had her suspicions, but she never let on. Someone in the church choir, I think. You know how you pick up little bits of conversations when you're a kid, and eventually you piece them together and make some sense of it all. Grandad and Grandma used to sing in the church choir, but, after he disappeared, she never went back to the church or the choir again – never had a good word to say about it. Quite the opposite. She really took against the church. God help the vicar if he ever came calling!"

"She was a feisty old bird."

"I thought you said she was a grumpy old cow."

"Same thing, isn't It?"

"Depends on your point of view, doesn't It?"

29th October 1964

I came to with the remnants of a nightmare nagging at the back of my brain. I could not work out if I was in or out of a dream. Had I just woken from one dream, only to find myself in the middle of another? I opened my eyes. I was back in the hospital waiting room. The old woman sat beside me, her red bonnet was still perched on her head, her leathered hand was holding mine. She smiled an empty smile, slipped her hand away and left the room without a word. Annoying bloody woman.

It was clear that this story, this dream, whatever it was, had to run its course. The inevitability of it was now more than mildly irritating. What is the point of reliving parts of your life if you cannot change the outcome?

The door opened again. Not the red bonnet this time. I leapt up. "Darling! Are you OK?" I heard myself saying. She looked awful; pale around the gills, her eyes bloodshot and distant.

"You'll need to sit down, pet," she said.

"Me? You're the one that needs to sit down. You look like death warmed up." I took her by the arm and settled her in the chair next to me.

"Doctor Sharp was right."

"Was he?" I said, struggling to pick up the conversation.

"I am pregnant." Her eyes lit up and she beamed the kind of smile that rarely touched her face anymore.

"But – "

"I know. And I'm geriatric apparently! Bloody rude, I call it. I've seen better days, I know......"

"But – "

"Don't worry, darling. I'll be alright. You're geriatric if you're over 35 in this game. The consultants explained some of the risks and he's looked through my notes and says I've got to take things easy, watch my blood pressure and the like, but he doesn't think there's any more risk for me than for anyone else of my age. We were just unlucky last time. It's not going to happen again."

I sat in silence. What could I say? 'You're right, darling. We will have a perfectly healthy boy. You'll blow up like a balloon and develop diabetes and a heart problem, and -'

"You're quiet. You are OK with this aren't you? We've talked about it." She placed her hands on mine. They felt warm and soothing.

"Do you still love me?" I asked.

"Of course, I do. What a thing to ask right now." She looked at me quizzically. "How long have we been married? 20 years? You're overweight, you never were much of a looker and you fart in bed – but we're still together, through thick and thin – more thick than thin some would say. So, yes, I still love you – and I haven't got any plans to stop real soon. Satisfied?"

"Yes. Am I enough for you?"

"Hey. Stop with the stupid questions, please. Now isn't the time." She leaned over and kissed me. "You're getting hormonal. It's not like you to get all emotional like this. That's my job. Come on. Let's go home."

So that's what we did. I was in a daze. She didn't stop talking the whole way. She was so excited. It was as though she knew somehow that this was going to be the one. By the time we'd walked out of the hospital she'd negotiated the whole gamut of potential names for both boys and girls. They had to be compatible with each other in case it turned out to be twins, which the consultant had assured her was a real possibility. The idea excited her. It was as if Jean and Joan had never existed. We walked down the hill to the bus station, listening to her plans for turning the box room in the new house into a nursery. By the time the bus had delivered us safely home, the paint and curtains had been selected and we were making plans for nursery school. I say we. She planned, I nodded and occasionally grunted in support or admiration as required.

Where had this new-found confidence come from? It was like having my old jenny wren back. I should have been rejoicing. I had worked out by now that my mood was dictated not by how I feel 'now', but by how I felt 'then'. I was not in control. I could do no more than feel the feelings that I felt at the time as each new event unfolded and slavishly repeat what had gone before. But there was a difference. Another part of my brain was interpreting the events, viewing them dispassionately and analysing every word and deed in a way that I had never done before. This was not a blessing. It was a curse. For the first time since this ordeal had begun, I started to long for the return of the old woman and her red bonnet. More than that. I wanted peace.

It was strange entering that house. I had walked out of it this morning to walk into town. The sun had been slanting low in the sky. It was Christmas Eve, a frosty chill in the air. A few houses sported Christmas wreaths on their front doors and, inside, decorations and Christmas trees were visible in almost every house. I had returned, this afternoon, in the Autumn. The streets were thick with golden leaves, but we were enjoying an Indian summer, basking in sunshine and weighing up the chances of taking our tea in the garden.

The daily paper told me it was October 1964. I walked around the house, taking in all that had changed in the last 3 years. It seemed spotlessly clean and tidy. We had been here less than 2 years by then and I'd recently finished decorating. We'd not had time to accumulate too much superfluous rubbish and the house was not yet redolent of nappy buckets and drying baby clothes.

The evening passed with more plans for our perfect life together with our future astronaut – or did we settle on Prime Minister? We went to bed. We snuggled, both wanting only the simple closeness of our bodies. Life appeared to move on as though the last 3 years had never happened. Perhaps they hadn't. Perhaps this was reality and my memories of our boy's birth and all the traumas that followed were the nightmare that haunted me. I lay there, darkness pressing in on me, too fearful to close my eyes in case the red bonnet would reappear and whisk me God knows where.

10th January 2018

"What are you doing?"

"Oh, hello Dad. Thought you were up the allotment."

"The ground was rock hard. Couldn't get the fork in. No point in staying."

"Never mind. There's always another day."

"And while the cat's away...."

"Oh this. I was just looking through some of the old photo albums."

"Why?"

"I wanted to see if I could find one of Grandad."

"I knew it would be something to do with that."

"It's alright. I'm not planning to take it to the police, or anything. I just wanted to see what he looked like."

"You won't let it rest will you."

"It's just – things don't seem to add up, that's all."

"Do they have to?"

"Granny and Grandad seemed so happy together - by all accounts. They always wanted a family. They had one for a while, and that was a sad time in their lives, but they lived through it all together and came out the other side just as much in love – stronger probably. Then they got exactly what they wanted, they got you, and you say it all fell apart. I don't understand why."

"And a photograph is going to help you understand, is It?"

"No, I suppose not. It will just help me picture them, that's all."

"You're still so young. You youngsters always want answers. As though everything can be explained by mathematics or science or statistics. It's not that easy, son. Sometimes things just happen. Shit happens. People do a thing for the oddest reason, or for no reason. You can't always understand why. We're not meant to."

"I hope you're not right, Dad. There's going to be a lot of frustrated coppers out there."

17th *June 1965*

I lay there with the darkness pressing in on me. Moments later, it seemed, I woke with a sharp elbow in my ribs and an insistent bellow echoing through my head.

"Get up – come on – get up! You can't lay there. Go and get the car started. I'll be down in two seconds." She grabbed a pile of clothes from the chair and headed for the bathroom. "Don't forget the bag. It's under the stairs!"

Half asleep and congenitally confused, even I could work out what was going on. The large wet stain spreading across the bedsheets was another clue, as though I needed one. It was June 1965. For the first time ever, she'd gone full term and we were about to experience the sort of frantic, middle-of-the-night dash to the hospital that most other couples could look back on fondly in their dwindling years. I threw on some clothes and hunted down the car key that I knew would be hanging on a hook by the front door. The slightly battered and very rusty Morris Minor Traveller that we'd bought only two months previously, for this very purpose, coughed and spluttered into life at only the third turn of the key. Thank God this was going to be a summer baby. If it had been the middle of winter, it could have been a different story. I pushed the choke in most of the way, conscious of not wanting to flood the car, and left it idling while I went back inside to shout up the stairs.

"Shake a leg, you scurvy layabout! Don't you know you've got a baby to deliver!" I could be calm and sensitive when it was really needed.

"We've got loads of time," she called, appearing at the top of the stairs holding her belly with both hands like she was carrying a heavy bucket of water. I took the stairs two at a time, stopping for breath only once, and escorted her down on my arm.

"Trust me, this one's going to be quick. Luckily, it's only 5 minutes to the hospital from here and you were very sensible to wait 'til 2 o'clock in the morning when the only traffic about is going to be coppers on speed patrol."

"You'll drive sensibly, won't you? I know you. The car will end up wrapped round a lamppost and the baby will be born halfway down the High Street."

"Trust me. I know what I'm doing," I said, with some confidence for once. I'd had a rehearsal.

I squeezed her into the car and threw her bag in the back. "That's the second time you've said that," she said, as I settled myself in the driving seat, crunched the gears and forgot to take the handbrake off. "Thanks. I do trust you." I wasn't sure how to take that, but it sounded like a compliment and I wasn't going to waste it.

"I love you. And I don't want you to be worried. You're going to be OK," I rambled, not sure where this was taking us.

"Watch the road please," she said, cool as a cucumber, as she stretched her hand out to steady herself on the dashboard. I narrowly avoided the kerb where a kink in the road suggested to most drivers that an avoiding strategy would be useful.

"See, we missed it." I turned my head to throw her one of my winning smiles and sailed through the red lights at the top of the High Street. The rest of the journey must have been uneventful. No policeman waved us down, there was no Presidential escort to the Maternity Wing. We simply turned up at the ante-natal ward, announced that we'd like some help with adding to the world over-population crisis and their well-oiled machine lumbered into joyless action. Why are midwives such cheerless creatures? I swear that half of them work a second shift at the meat factory every night. There is a conveyor belt efficiency to childbirth that relies on mothers being treated like beasts of the field and fathers with cold indifference. I waited for one of them to tell me that I'd done my bit and the best thing I could do was to sit quietly in the waiting room or, better still, go home and not come back until the excitement was over. I did not have long to wait.

"Are you the father?" said a large person sporting a blue skirt, a bloodied apron and a five o'clock shadow.

"I hope so," I said, "unless you know differently."

"Wait in there," she barked, "and don't come out."

As a navy man, these were instructions I could understand. "Yes Chief." I saluted, about turned as smartly as my slippers would allow, and marched to my post. I don't think she appreciated the joke.

Less than 20 minutes later, Dr Sharp joined me in the waiting room, looming over me like an elongated vulture waiting to pick my bones. If I'd known then what I know now, I would have beaten the living daylights out of him, there and then. And now, I do know what I didn't know then – so why didn't I belt him as soon as he stepped into the room? Frustration was building up inside me but there was nothing I could do. I was trapped inside this kaleidoscope of memories, impotent, unable to break myself away from their inevitable conclusion.

I sat like a dummy listening to his patient explanation. He just happened to be seeing in another emergency admission. He'd seen my wife come in. He wanted to let me know that, as he was her GP, he would be honoured to deliver our baby himself! The lying bastard. God, how I wanted to push his teeth down the back of his throat.

My head must have nodded. He actually put his hand on my shoulder and said, "I can see that you're concerned about her, but please don't worry. I have a lot of obstetrics experience and I know your wife's medical history very well...(I'll say he bloody well did!)...She couldn't be in any better hands." He smiled at me and left the room. The fucking little toe rag actually smiled at me.

10th January 2018

"He wasn't much like you, was he?"

"What's that?"

"Grandad. I found it in one of the old photo albums."

"Bloody hell. I've not seen that in many a year. Dapper little fellow, wasn't he?"

"No-one looks like that now. Look at him. Proper raincoat neatly folded over one arm, felt hat at a jaunty angle. He looks like something out of a Gene Kelly movie."

"What do you know about Gene Kelly? You're much too young."

"Come off it. The number of times you made me watch 'Singing in the Rain'? I knew that film off by heart before I started primary school. When do you think it was taken?"

"Soon after the war probably; early 50s maybe. I wonder who took it? He's outside the Bull Inn - look. Maybe your Grandma took it. She worked there for a while."

"I can't see her as a barmaid."

"She was a cook. A damn good one. She always said she wished she didn't cook such good dinners. He wouldn't have got so fat."

"He was skinny when this was taken."

"He was. He looked a bit like Norman Wisdom, didn't he?"

"Which is odd."

"Why?"

"Well, you look more like Tommy Cooper."

"Yeah, very funny."

"You're tall though. And Grandma wasn't very big either. You got some tall genes from somewhere."

"They grew up in the 20s remember, and then they had years of rationing. It was no wonder they didn't grow much. Do you feel better now?"

"I'm OK."

"Now you've found a picture."

"It would be nice to find one of them together."

"I don't think there are any. She threw them all out."

28th June 1965

The fucking little toe rag actually smiled at me. I stood there, seething inside for God knows how long. The door opened again and she came in, red bonnet bobbing up and down like one of Santa's elves. She was excited about something. She held the door open a little wider and my family followed her into the room. My new family. There had been some brief, unseen, unheard rent in time, yet again. My bowling ball wife had been replaced by a small, glowing angel with a tiny, blue-eyed cherub in her arms.

There were tears in her eyes. Tears of joy I hoped. "Take us home," she said quietly. My guardian was still holding the door open, hopping from foot to foot and beaming wider than the Eddystone Lighthouse. She thrust my wife's overnight bag into my hand and followed us out. We negotiated the corridors and stairs that we knew so well and stepped out into bright sunshine. In front of us, the beaten up taxi and its beaten up driver waited with their engines running. All five of us slid in, with much clutching of baby's head and a 'hold on tight now', as though we were mounting a Blackpool tram.

The trip home was all too familiar. The river, running brown and sluggish, buses pulling out from the station without a care, the High Street, bustling with shoppers bent on spending every penny of last week's pay packet. The old lady sat in front of us, taking in every word and movement. Could my jenny wren not see her there? She took no notice of her; gave no acknowledgement that she could see her at all.

St. Francis' tall spire loomed ahead of us. How I longed for Daphne now, for the cool silence of the church, for peace and time to think, but we swept past. The old lady watched me, watching the receding church, but gave no indication that she knew what was in my heart.

We arrived at our little terraced house in next to no time and baby was soon tucked into his non-committal, lemon-yellow cot in his yellow bedroom with sun and flower stencils decorating the walls – the room that would be blue with dinosaurs and robots before the month was out.

"Did you pay the taxi driver?"

I went downstairs and out of the front door. I knew it was pointless. They wouldn't be there.

18th May 1966

They weren't. I turned to go back indoors but it was shut. I hadn't shut it - had I? I knocked the door and it was opened almost straight away. She had changed. She was wearing a pair of dungarees I couldn't remember seeing before, their shapeless form concealing the post-birth body that, this time, could not regain its former glory. Her hair, normally shoulder length and free, was now tied to her head in a tight bun. Her cheeks flushed pink. A nappy-pin was clenched between her teeth.

"Forget your key again?" she sprayed, turning to trot back into the living room.

He was downstairs now, more than twice the size and rolling on a blanket in the middle of the floor, boldly displaying his manliness, at least for a few more seconds, until a clean nappy was located and folded into place with dexterous fingers. "Make yourself useful," she said, holding out a dirty nappy, pinched between finger and thumb. "You're better at this bit than me." I took it to the kitchen and used my special navy training to push the shitty contents down the sink and toss the nappy in the bucket to soak.

I was washing my hands when she came up behind me and put her hands around my waist. "You OK, love. You've been a bit quiet the last couple of weeks."

"I'm fine."

"You sure? You sure you didn't ought to go and see the doctor?" She must have felt the tightening in my chest and guessed how it reflected in my face. "Don't look like that. You might just need a tonic or something. Dr. Sharp says it's quite common in – "

"Dr. Sharp?" I turned to look at her.

"I saw him this morning."

"Again? I thought you only had to see him once a month."

"I do. He was in the clinic this morning, when I was weighing baby... You don't mind, do you? Asking for you? I said you ought to make an appointment, but you didn't seem to be doing anything about it."

"I'm fine," I said. "I don't need to see a doctor. It's busy at work, I'm not getting a decent night's sleep and I'm tired, that's all." I turned back to the sink in the hope of finding something interesting there. "The last thing I need is some quack doctor giving me pick-me-ups."

27th February 2018

"Today's paper"

"Oh, thanks."

"Page 5."

"What?"

"I think you should read it."

"Read it to me. I'm busy not being arsed."

"Dad! Where do you pick up this language? You're a bad influence on the younger generation - that's me, by the way.   Ready? 'An inquest was held today - that's yesterday I guess - into the circumstances surrounding the discovery of a 50-year old skeleton on the site of the Workhouse Fields development. A thorough investigation of the area and the remains, and a local appeal for information to assist the police with their enquiries, have failed to conclude who the unfortunate individual might be, or how the body came to be there. The Coroner had no option but to declare an open verdict. A spokesman for the police, Detective Inspector Baldwin, said that, in the light of certain information, which he and the Coroner were not at liberty to reveal, the case would remain open pending further enquiries'. What do you make of that?"

"At a guess I'd say the Coroner couldn't give a damn one way or the other, and Baldock – "

"Baldwin."

"Baldwin – couldn't detect a turd in a perfume factory."

12th November 1965

"I'm going out for a walk."

"You've only just come home."

I turned to her and spoke with unnecessary venom. "I want to be alone." I headed for the door, grabbing my coat as I swept through the hallway.

"Alone with who, I wonder," she threw at my retreating back.

"Not bloody Dr. Sharp for a start," I yelled as I slammed the front door.

I stood there for a moment, trying to work out what had just happened. Was that one argument or all of them rolled together? If I went back in the house now, would I be there on the same day, at the same time, or would time have moved forward again? What should I do now? Slavishly, I waited for a red-bonnet to hove into view, or for an ancient taxi to take me to my next destination? My feet found their own way, kicking through fallen Autumn leaves. I was heading towards the town centre without knowing why or where I was heading. I felt lost and very, very alone – lonely, that is so much worse.

Seconds later, it seemed, I was pushing open the creaking door of St. Francis'. Was this a Wednesday? Was it even the afternoon? I had no idea. I was too exhausted to care. I sat in my usual pew, clasped my hands together and begged for relief from this purgatory. I did not hear her come in or feel her sit beside my but when her hand brushed mine, I realised that Daphne had arrived and that she was holding out a tissue for my streaming eyes. I must have smiled or said something appropriate.

"That's better," she said. "I've missed you. It looks like you've been having a rough time."

I could barely talk. Not coherently at least. I tried to tell her that I felt I was in a dream, that my thoughts were not my own anymore, that I was constantly reliving episodes of my life, most of which I'd rather forget. That most of the time I wanted to be alone and yet I couldn't bear the loneliness. Part of my brain told me I could not be saying these things if I was still inside my nightmare, but I was making no sense to myself, and surely less to her. She was calm. She was always calm. She said she thought I might be suffering from post-baby blues. I thought she was joking, trying to break through my confusion by saying something - anything. But no, she was serious. Her husband had told her all about it.

"He's known plenty of men with it," she said. "It usually happens about 3 to 6 months after the baby's born. It's about 4 or 5 months for you now, isn't it? It's depression and it's very real. You should go and see your doctor."

Great. Now there were two of them on my case. "Maybe," I said.

"Please do, I'm worried about you." Her hand clasped mine gently and I rested my hand on her arm, but she flinched and pulled away. She got up. "Go home. You need your family round you at a time like this." With a parting smile, she left through the vestry, gathering her broom and dusters on the way.

When I heard the church door creak behind me, I knew exactly who it was.

13th February 2018

"It's freezing out there! Shift over Dad, I need to see some of that radiator."

"Where have you been?"

"Down the library."

"Haven't we got enough books as it is?"

"I was reading newspapers. They've got copies of The Gazette going back to before the war."

"So?"

"I wanted to look at 1967, 1968, see if there was anything about Grandad."

"Like a bloody Rottweiler you, aren't you? What did you find?"

"Nothing. Disappointing really. A man goes missing, you'd think someone would find that interesting."

"I wouldn't."

"Lots of stuff about the new hospital being built and that flower power festival up at Victoria Park, you know, when they brought in the police with their horses and dogs. Some woman was arrested for walking down the High Street, starkers, throwing rose petals at the shoppers!"

"Yeah, that's more the sort of thing that interests me."

"It all went on in your day, Dad."

"Before my time, son, more's the pity. Biggest thing I can remember happening in this town when I was a youngster was Duran Duran appearing at the Civic Hall."

"Who?"

27ᵗʰ February 1967

I knew exactly who it was. She stood there, framed in the open doorway; snow falling in heavy lumps behind her, snowflakes littering her bonnet and cape. The cape was a new feature. I'd not seen that before. I expected a beckoning finger to wheedle out from under it but, instead, she stepped inside, closed the door, shook the snow from her cloak and came to sit by me. She looked at me pityingly and seemed about to speak but thought better of it.

"Who are you?" I asked, never expecting an answer, so not being disappointed when the only response was her slightly disturbing smile. She just pulled the cloak around her knees and shuffled sideways to one end of the pew. The vestry door opened and Daphne returned. She propped her broom in the corner and smoothed down the housecoat that she always wore in here. She looked so different. Her hair was short, no longer vibrant and golden. It was, at best, dirty blond, hovering close to mousy brown, and flattened to her head with hairgrips. She looked tired. Black bags under her eyes betrayed sleepless nights, her skin was pale and sallow, ageing her by 10 years. She looked up and seemed briefly shocked to see me.

"Hello. I though you weren't ever coming back. I haven't seen you in here for months." She slid in next to me, ignoring the old lady watching from the other end of the pew. "How are feeling now?"

"I'm OK," I said automatically. "I wish I could say as much for you. You don't look well."

"Oh, don't worry about me," she said firmly. "Just a touch of 'flu. Nothing that a pools win and six months in the Bahamas couldn't fix. I heard about your job. Sorry."

"My job? Oh – I see..." It registered that she'd heard I'd been made redundant. So, it must be later than January 1967 now. We'd somehow skipped forward again. When did we get all that snow, last week of February? "Yes, I'm on the scrap heap now. We're all being replaced with machines, hadn't you heard? You'll be next. I hear someone's developing an electric duster."

"They're called Hoovers. We've had them for years. I can see you don't do a lot of housework."

"Did you miss me?" I don't know where that question came from or why I asked it.

"Yes." She stood up quickly, wincing as a pain seemed to shoot through her body. "I must get on. This new vicar's a tartar. He won't like it If he sees me fraternising with the customers."

"You OK? Are you in pain?"

"It's nothing."

"It doesn't look like nothing." I said pointing at the yellowed edge of a large bruise, just visible at the cuff of her blouse.

"I tripped – took a bit of a bump. Honestly, it's nothing. I'm always bumping into things and tripping over my own feet." For the first time ever, I couldn't believe her. I thought I knew her. She had never hidden anything from me before, but the look in her eyes told a story different to the one she was telling me. "Please, don't worry about me." Before I could say more, she fled through the vestry door, leaving her broom propped in the corner.

I felt the pew rock slightly as the old woman rose, tying the silk ribbons of her bonnet firmly under her chin. I followed. She opened the ancient church door and we stepped out into a chill winter evening.

27th February 2018

"The new hospital was opened by Princess Anne. Did you know that?"

"No. Now ask me if I care."

"How did you get to be such an old grouch? I'm not going to be like that when I'm –"

"Old?"

"Your age."

"Old."

"It took 10 years to build and various bits were transferred from the old hospital to the new one a bit at a time. Maternity was one of the – "

"Are we spending the whole of the rest of the day on a history lesson?"

"It's interesting. I'm trying to work out how Grandad could have ended up on the old hospital site. He disappeared on Christmas Eve 1967. The old hospital closed for good in February 1967 and the Ministry of Agriculture moved into some of the main buildings in 1970, but they were only there for 3 years, and It's been derelict ever since."

"I've never understood that. The place has been a bloody eyesore for most of my life."

"Some weird planning covenant or other, I think. Something to do with the Town Council going back to the days when it was a workhouse. Couldn't really follow it to be honest."

"So, I can see how maybe he got in – or was taken in – who knows what actually happened – but anyway, he got in when it was a derelict building. But how come nobody found the body when the Ministry of Agriculture was there?"

"Well, you know Civil Servants. They're all a bunch of stiffs anyway. Dead from the neck up, most of them. I guess one more stiff sat in the corner didn't get noticed."

"He must have been buried."

"I don't think so. You've got to read between the lines because the police reports have been a bit sketchy, but they said some workers 'stumbled over him' in some sort of derelict outhouse. I think if they'd dug him up, they would have said."

27th February 1967

We stepped out into a chill winter evening, and there, standing right in front of us, was my wife. My little jenny wren, looking more and more each day like the chief petty officer who'd made my life hell on HMS Ceylon.

"So, there you are!" she bellowed. "I've been looking everywhere for you. You're meant to be at home looking after the baby. I'm the one who's supposed to be here. I've got choir practice. Here, take him. God knows where your head is these days." She thrust the pushchair at me and with a final glare, pushed past me into the church. We walked home alone. No sign of the woman or her red bonnet or her cape. Just two lonely, silent soles making tracks in the snow.

I fed him and put him to bed. He was no trouble. He rarely was. He wasn't even two yet, but I liked to read him a story at bedtime. I wanted him to know the sound of my voice, perhaps to have some deep-seated memory of our time together. I was already fearful that our perfect marriage was heading towards a rocky shore and that I couldn't navigate a safe course away from the inevitable shipwreck.

She returned home in as foul a mood as I remembered. I had no doubt that there would be no reprieve, no miraculous skip in time that would let me avoid reliving this fateful night. Bitterness and disappointment tumbled out in words of regret and accusation. Why was I never here? Why wasn't I out finding another job? Why was I such a useless father? Why wasn't I someone else? I wanted to fight back, but there was no strength in me to do it. I had no words that I could muster in my defence, and I could not hit her. I could not hit anyone, least of all her. She deserved so much more than this. I had no explanation for how I felt or why I was acting the way I was. A darkness had overtaken me. I no longer had any control. Her haranguing went on for 10 more minutes, until the baby was crying in his bed upstairs and the neighbours were thumping the wall. It was when she said that she would call Dr Sharp the next morning that I flipped. Why him? Why not my doctor – Hepburn? Why did everything come back to that gangling string-bean?

Suddenly, I let rip. I did not know I had such anger in me. I pushed her back against the kitchen dresser. Plates and cups spilled out, smashing and splintering across the floor. I demanded to know what was going on. Why did she see so much of him? What was so special about him? Why did every conversation start and end with Dr. fucking Sharp?! I tried to stop it happening again but there was nothing I could do. My hands were round her throat before I knew it.

"Why does our baby have blue eyes?"

"Wha – "

"You have brown eyes. I have brown eyes. Why does our baby have blues eyes?! Blue eyes like Sharp's." But she was a jenny. They bred them tough. She must have thought it was a typical Friday night down The Crown and Anchor in Portsmouth all those years ago. One quick knee to the bollocks was all it took to turn me into a whimpering child.

Panting, she slid to the floor to join me. We stared at each other for a few seconds – minutes – I don't know. Our marriage reduced to a slanging match, a glaring match, both on our knees, surrounded by shards of broken crockery. "What is going on with you? Are you on drugs or something? Do you think I have the time, let alone the inclination, to go chasing after someone else? Are you mad?!" She wasn't wrong, of course. I wept, and then I screamed, and then, I think, I wept some more.

What time elapsed between then and the ambulance, I could not tell. My memory was as hazy the second time around as it was the first. I remember rocking in the corner of the kitchen, hushed voices and our son's cries echoing round my head. There were neighbours and a policeman, and two large men with a stretcher that didn't get used. Some clarity returned as my weary carcass hit the crisp night air. I was guided between two burly ambulance drivers, a blanket draped around my shoulders. The least surprising thing was the sight of the old lady in her bright red bonnet sitting in the back of the ambulance as I was gently welcomed into its nurturing warmth.

We sat in silence for a few minutes, me, the medic and the old woman, but as we drove past the Odeon and the imposing, red-brick edifice of the hospital beckoned us, I asked, "Why are you doing this to me?"

"It's for your own good," said the burly medic. "They can check you over. Give you something to calm you down."

"I wasn't talking to you," I said. He just smiled at me –
indulgently.

7th March 2018

Detective Inspector Baldwin sat in his tiny cubicle-cum-office staring at the ancient, borrowed whiteboard that was propped up on the filing cabinet in front of him. Red, green and blue pens had been employed to mark out different aspects of the case, but, as it was some weeks since he'd looked at it, he was struggling to remember what those aspects were. There were a few random dates, a corner dedicated to the 'scene of crime' and a list of items found there, all linked by badly joined lines, some dotted, some partially rubbed away. He would have to start again.

Three court hearings, two budget meetings, orders from on high to put together a PowerPoint presentation on 'crime prevention in primary schools' and catching up on the last six months' returns for the Management Information Team had put paid to any progress on real detecting. He opened the sealed plastic bag on the desk in front of him and spilled the contents onto his blotter, letting the fates decide how they fell. His phone jangled for the seventeenth time that morning. "Morning Barry, I hope I find you well. This is your friendly Customer Facing Communications Executive at your service."

"Piss off."

"Your feedback is duly noted and has been recorded for future ref - " Barry replaced the receiver. It rang again in seconds.

"Solly, long number," said DI Baldwin, in what he hoped passed for a comedic Fu Manchu imitation.

"Christ Barry, what was that? You do realise I should report you for contravening the diversity code? Stop pissing about now. I've got a boy down here wants to speak to someone who knows what's going on with the hospital case. I told them that no such person exists but, in an emergency, they could talk to you, and they took the bait."

"I'll come down."

"Better still, I'll send him up. I don't want good-looking, fresh-faced young men littering my front desk. It's bad for my image. I'm expecting some real criminals to come in and hand themselves over to justice at any minute."

Five minutes later a PCSO of no fixed gender led a young lad into Baldwin's cubicle, pulled out a chair for him and asked if either of them would like a cup of tea of coffee. They both looked about 12 years old, but at least one of them ought to be somewhat older. Baldwin couldn't remember when anyone in this office had last offered to make him a drink and made a mental note to invite more visitors up here.

"What can I do for you, young man?"

"I think that body you found is my Grandad. He disappeared and when he didn't come back my Grandma thought he'd gone off with another woman, but nobody knew who she was, and I don't think it's true and, anyway the dates are just too weird, and I think you ought to see this..."

"Whoa, whoa. Try slowing down a bit. We'll take things one at a time, shall we? When did your Grandad go missing? Have you been asked to complete a missing person's report?"

"1967. Christmas Eve, 1967. But look at this...."

"One thing at a time. Was he reported missing?"

"I don't know. It was 30 years before I was born. I don't think so. Hey, are those all his things?"

Baldwin took a long slurp at his coffee and looked into the boyish face of the young man in front of him, his eyes wide and excited like a five-year-old on an Easter egg hunt. Was he just another glory hunter?

27th February 1967

The burly medic smiled at me indulgently. "Perhaps I should give you a shot of this," he said, producing an unnecessarily large and imposing syringe.

"What's that?"

"Just a little morphine solution."

"I'm not in pain."

"You will be when I stick this in you," he said, suddenly looking deadly earnest. His face broke into a wide smile. "I'm just kidding with you. You will feel a tiny prick. It'll help to calm you down."

I don't remember arriving at the hospital.

7th *March 2018*

"So, this is the coffee he bought. It's one of our family heirloom stories – the day Grandpa went out to buy coffee and never came back."

"That's interesting."

"Yes, and Grandma apparently never drank coffee again 'til the day she died."

"I was thinking more that it was interesting you knew it was coffee, but then I suppose it was in the paper."

"We saw it on Facebook."

"The fount of all knowledge."

"Yeah, I know, but it was the thing that caught my eye. And the dates tied up. There's no label. How do you know the sell-by date?"

"Marks and Spencer is a very efficient company. There's a code pressed into the bottom of the glass, look. M & S were the first company to do that - just for their own purposes. Then they started putting actual dates on labels so customers could see them, and other companies followed suit. They weren't in common use 'til the 70s."

"You struck lucky."

"Not as lucky as when we found the guy who still had all the records stashed in a vault. He told us exactly what was in the jar, when it was made, who their suppliers were. Just about everything except what the delivery driver had for breakfast. Sometimes you can have information overload. Don't touch anything please."

"Sorry. I wanted to take a look at the knife. Will we get this stuff back – when you've finished with it?"

"Get it back? You're saying it's yours, are you?"

"Well, my Grandad's, yeah."

"You've got a lot more explaining to do yet, lad. A lot more." DI Baldwin opened a draw, pulled out a thick pad and dropped it on the desk with a satisfying thud. "I'm going to ask you lots of questions. You're going to give me lots of answers and if all you do is repeat a load of guff you read on Facebook, I will charge you with wasting police time. If I think you might be genuine, maybe we'll think about putting it all down as a witness statement – in triplicate. I do hope you've got plenty of time to spare."

1ˢᵗ April 1967

The next time I opened my eyes, I was in a hospital bed. They must have thought I was someone important. I was in a side room, all by myself. Bright sun streamed through a large window to my right. I lay there for some minutes, watching millions of tiny dust particles caught in the sun's rays, trying to make sense of things. I couldn't. I barely knew where to start. It was some minutes before it even occurred to me that this could now be reality. Had I been taken to hospital for some unknown reason, and in my drugged stupor, had I been dreaming?

No, even drowsy and disorientated, I knew this room was familiar. This was not my 'today'. This was no winter sun that flooded the room with bright light. The birdsong I could hear sang of spring, of yellow flowers decorating the countryside, welcoming new life to the fields and hedgerows.

The door opened and a trolley wheeled in, closely followed by a tall, red-headed nurse in a starched, white uniform. She was crisp, from her perfectly placed, startlingly white hat to her gleaming patent leather shoes. She smiled crisply. "You're awake." Observant too – she would go far. "That's good. It will make giving your medicines so much easier. How are you feeling? Refreshed? Ready to face the troubles of the day? The consultant will be along shortly to check you over. How's your temperature?" The final comment was said whilst grabbing my chin and thrusting a thermometer under my tongue. Her questions were clearly not intended to be answered. Not by me at least. While the thermometer did its patient work, she shook a plethora of tablets from as many pots into a tiny paper container. Each new tablet came with a brief, gleeful explanation of what it could do to me, but I was in no mood to take it in. She extracted the thermometer with one hand and glanced at it disdainfully, while filling a cup on the bedside cabinet with water from a battered metal jug with the other hand and barely pausing for breath. "You have been out for a long time. Wish I could sleep that long. Perhaps I should be taking some of these. Now then, they've all got to go down. I hope you're not going to be funny about taking pills. I have lots of other patients to look after, you know. Come on, down in one." She had tossed the thermometer aside and now held out the cup in one hand and my little pot of happy pills in the other.

"Will they put me to sleep again?"

"I certainly hope not. I have to give you a bed bath in half an hour and I want you fully conscious."

"I shall look forward to that," I said, "Pat. I take it that is your name and not an instruction."

She glanced down at the name tag perched on her crisp, white breast. "I can see there's nothing much wrong with you," she said and, wheeling her trolley in the general direction of her next victim, made a haughty exit.

I sunk back into the warm, inviting bed. Two minutes of forced banter had taken a lot out of me. I felt drained, but I had avoided the obvious, inane question, 'where am I?' I knew where I was; the County Mental Hospital.

I awoke sometime later to find a mad professor prodding me in the shoulder. Pat, the starched nurse stood at his shoulder, daring me to misbehave, employing her eyebrows and her expertly folded arms.

The mad professor was no height at all. I am shorter than average, but I might have towered over this guy. He wore a double-breasted blazer with gold piping at the lapels. He looked like a tiny sea captain except that his silk cravat, half-moon glasses and frizzy, curly white hair clearly marked him out as an eccentric academic. When he started talking like one of Enid Blyton's jolly rotten foreigners, the likeness was complete.

"I am most sorry to disturb you, but I need to discuss with you your meanings for being here. Let me introduce myself. I am Valentin von Rothschild. You may call me Max."

"Hi Max." Should I ask the obvious question?

"First must we establish what you think you are here about."

"What?"

"That is right. Vot."

This was going to be a hard slog and I didn't think I had the energy.

7th March 2018

Six cups now occupied much of the precious space on DI Baldwin's desk. A face appeared around the corner and asked, "More coffee?"

"No thanks, but you can take this lot away and wash them up."

"Above my pay grade, I'm afraid," and the face disappeared.

Temporarily lost for words, Baldwin stared at the tightly packed wordage on the pad in front of him and tried to piece together the slightly rambling tale it told. He still had unanswered questions but from what he'd heard so far, on the face it, it sounded like the boy's Grandad was a good candidate for a match. Perhaps a DNA check could be arranged. They were much cheaper these days and, right now, he wasn't on the Super's blacklist, so he could probably get her to sign it off.

"I forgot all about this." Baldwin's visitor pulled a worn brown envelope out of his inside coat pocket and rummaged around in its contents.

"It's not a suicide note is it?"

"No, no," he carefully smoothed out a large, worn and slightly browned document over the top of the witness statement he'd recently signed. "His birth certificate."

"That's OK. If you tell me he was born on Christmas Eve, I'm happy to believe you. I don't need proof."

"It's not that." He pointed to the first box.

"Yes, I can see it - 24th December 1917."

"No, underneath that. Look, 'When and where born'. Union House, Warren Road."

"So?"

"It was a workhouse. By 1917 it had its own infirmary. Lots of babies were born there."

"I don't doubt it."

"It became a hospital in the 1930s." There was a long pause while the two men stared at the certificate, and each other, neither wanting to be the first to say the actual words.

"Did I tell you I don't believe in coincidences?" Baldwin reached for one of the coffee cups, registered that it was empty, and returned it carefully.

"He was born on Christmas Eve, 1917, disappeared, died we think, exactly 50 years later, on Christmas Eve, 1967, and then, 50 years later, he's found on Christmas Eve, 2017 – in the very building he was born in. That's spooky."

DI Baldwin stared long and hard at nothing in particular.

"You OK? My Dad didn't really want me to do this. He said I'd be wasting your time. This is just too weird though. I needed to share it with someone. I'm right, aren't I? It's too weird."

"There could be more to this."

"That's what I said. There could be more to this than meets the eye. Why that day? What's special about that place? Dad didn't want me talking to you. He doesn't believe in coincidences either. He'd rather everybody just forgot about – "

"Stop talking." He stopped talking. There were a few seconds of silence. A telephone rang somewhere at the other end of the room and Baldwin waited for it to be picked up before he spoke again. "This also interests me." His finger hovered over a box near the middle of the long, thin document. *"Signature, description and residence of informant.* A relative of yours?" He spun the certificate round to face the young man, who frowned and shook his head. *"Ethel Snooks, Matron, Union House, Warren Road."*

"Funny name."

"Not a name you'd forget in a hurry. There's something else."

"What?"

"This certificate is dated the same day as the birth, 24th December. That's unusual."

"Impossible?"

"No, just unusual. Of course, registrars used to visit the hospitals in those days. Must have just happened to be there that day." Baldwin drifted off into his thoughts. The boy coughed politely.

"I don't suppose that – "

"Have you ever taken the Midnight Ghost Walk?"

"What's that?"

"You live in this town and you've never heard of the Ghost Walk? You need to get out more. Once a month the Museum Curator does a guided tour of the town. Starts at the Town Hall at midnight and takes in all the town's ghostly locations."

"I didn't know there were any."

"Oh yes. There's the girl in brown at the Coach and Horses, the headless cavalier in the castle grounds, loads of them, but the highlight of the night's entertainment is the mysterious Ethel Snooks."

"I've never heard of her."

"Charles Snooks was the infamous Master of the workhouse. He ruled it with an iron fist in an iron glove, by all accounts. His wife, Ethel, was the Matron. Discipline in workhouses was always tough, but Union House was said to be one of the worst. And Charles Snooks had some, shall we say, exotic interests, especially when it came to small boys. They say that more than one person died at the hands of Charles and Ethel Snooks – men, women and children, they didn't care. The rumours were that Ethel, would procure young children, even babies, to satisfy Charles' unusual tastes. She was, I suppose, the closest thing the town had to a midwife. It was never proved, of course. Hundreds of deaths, and births probably, went unrecorded in the workhouse in those days."

"And now Ethel's a ghost?"

"She is seen most often prowling the streets on – on her rounds, usually dressed in her red cape and her bonnet."

"How did she die?"

"Strangled to death - with her bonnet – by her husband."

"The sadistic bastard."

"In the Great War, the workhouse got commandeered as a military hospital. The Master's house was used as a billet for the officers. Charles and Ethel found themselves sleeping in the cellars. One of the officers found them one morning."

"Found them? Like in, found them both dead?"

"They think he'd strangled her. She was found hanging from a metal grating with her bonnet so tightly wrapped around her neck it had almost severed it. He'd cut his own throat with a razor. Speculation was that she'd had enough of him, or got pangs of remorse, and had threatened to turn him in. We'll never know the full story now."

"So that would have happened around the time Grandad was born."

DI Baldwin grimaced and reached for the phone. It took only seconds for him to be put through to the local museum and in less than a minute he was talking to the curator. "Hello. I am Detective Inspector Baldwin. We met.......oh, do you?.......I'm investigating – well, could you just answer a quick question for me? Charles and Ethel Snooks. Can you remind me exactly when they were found?"

The grandson leaned forward, hoping to make some sense of the muffled responses.

"Yes, yes, I'm familiar with the story. I was just hoping you could tell me when their bodies were discovered......Yes, you're right, I'm sure, we should know that, but by the time I even find a requisition form for the blokes in Archives, you could just tell me.......I have done the tour and I don't want to have to do it again........Just tell, me the bloody date!....... Thank you." He put the phone down and made a mental note to find out what car the Museum Curator drove and fill out a stolen car report for it.

His pen was poised over a sticky-note that he had peeled off to jot the date down, but he thought better of it."

"Well?"

"Not especially. You'll recall that a couple of eons ago I told you I don't believe in coincidences?"

"Yes."

"That is still very much the case."

"But what's the date?"

"Christmas Day, 1917. – but they'd almost certainly died some hours earlier – probably the previous evening."

"Christmas Eve."

1st April 1967

I felt so drained. "Must we do this now?"

"You have been here for a month now. It's about time you started to co-operate." Pat, the crisply turned out nurse glared at me like a Victorian school mistress.

"A month? I don't remember."

"How convenient for you," she said. "You were so violent when you first came in that we had to keep you confined and sedated."

"I don't – "

"You have been in this room for almost a week and you have slept for most of that time. It's time you started to face up to reality."

This girl could do with a lesson or two in bedside manners.

"No-one here wishes to make you more pressure, but if we are to be helping with you, we must talk much." The mad professor was peering at me over the foot of the bed. This pair should be on the stage. They'd go down a storm at The Palladium. "I am a psychologist. Do you understand what is that?"

"I'd kind of guessed that. Did she put me in here?"

"She? Your wife perhaps?" The professor squinted at me as though he'd left his monocle at home.

"Who else?"

"Many peoples have agreed that you should be better here with us. Yes, your wife, but also too the polizei and the social workers and the doctor."

"Which doctor?" Mini-Max looked to the nurse for help and she referred to her clipboard.

"Dr. Sharp. Dr. Paul Sharp."

"I want to see my wife."

"That is not of the best ideas."

"I want to see my wife – now." I threw off the bedclothes with a vague idea of finding her.

"Get back in that bed now," barked Pat, shoving me back down with one hand strategically placed on my chest while she grabbed an ankle with the other. These nurses were better trained in jujitsu than I'd been as a Royal Navy commando. We could have done with her on the beaches in Burma.

"How long have you had these violent tendencies?" asked the grim-face Professor. "Do you often make violent thoughts towards your wife?"

"I never have violent thoughts towards my wife. I love my wife. Why isn't she here? She never comes in to see me. Is she alright?"

"She is recovering." The look on Pat's face was not conducive to more banter.

"What do you mean?"

"She is not ready to see you yet. Her eye socket has not fully healed, her ribs are still painful, and she will never get back the teeth you knocked out."

"Teeth? I don't understand?"

"Another convenient lapse of memory?"

The professor coughed politely. "The brain is a remarkable thing. Perhaps, this is a memories you are wishing to suppress."

"I don't understand. She was fine. We argued, and I think she threw some plates, but – "

"It wasn't just an argument, was it?" If Nurse Pat had a knuckle-duster, she'd have been polishing it by now. "I've seen the marks on her neck."

"Her neck?" I sank back into the bed. "I don't – "

The mad professor gathered his papers together. "'We shall continue this conversation at another days." He turned to Nurse Pat and addressed her left breast while adjusting the focus on his glasses. "We call this the stage of denial. It will pass in time. I think the time is right for the group therapies."

"We'll start him off with basket weaving tomorrow."

I closed my eyes.

8th March 2018

"You did what?!"

"Calm down, Dad. You won't do your blood pressure any good."

"I specifically said to you that I didn't want to involve the police!"

"I know, Dad, but can't you see, this is a chance to find some answers – to put a line under – "

"I don't want to put a fucking line under it!"

12th April 1967

I might have been a basket case, but I knew it wouldn't last forever. The one good thing about reliving past experiences is that you know the outcome, that the light at the end of the tunnel is not always on oncoming train, that being powerless is sometimes easier to cope with.

She was there again, sitting in my one armchair, rocking slightly, looking more like Madame Defarge each time I saw her. She never talks, just watches, and smiles – grimaces – her red bonnet bobbing to and fro.

There was a tap on the door. I don't know why she knocked. I was expecting her. She knew I was expecting her.

"Come in." The door opened tentatively. "I don't bite."

"Hello," she said, pushing the door closed quietly as though she was fearful of waking someone in the next room. She looked as beautiful as ever. "You look well." She sounded a little surprised, maybe even disappointed.

"They're looking after me. Plenty of fresh fruit and vegetables; the odd Guinness when I'm a good boy."

"That sounds good."

"I've only had one." She smiled. That made me feel better. We stared at each other for a few seconds, neither knowing how to move the conversation on. "I like the nose."

"All the girls are wearing them like this now. It's the latest fashion." It was only very slightly out of kilter. I might be the only person who'd notice. There was a faint yellow tinge in the corner of one eye but no other evidence that she'd been in the wars.

"I'm sorry."

"I know." She smiled again, and it looked convincing. "Where do we go from here?" she asked.

"Home please. I don't want to be here anymore."

"Are you bored? That's a good sign. It might mean you're ready to face the world again."

"How could I be bored? Look at my hands. I'm weaving baskets from morning 'til night. Next week, I progress to mailbags, and if I get on well with that, they might promote me to rock breaking."

"Can I join your escape committee?"

"I'd like that." There was another one of those slightly awkward moments. "I need to be sure I'd be welcome at home."

"Of course you would," she said, "and there's a little boy who's getting desperate to see his Daddy."

"Really?"

"Yes, really."

There was a creak from the armchair in the corner. "Ignore her," I said, "the old hag's been sitting there all morning like the condemned man's jailor, not saying a word. She won't bother you."

"Do you mind?!" I snapped my head round at the unexpected comment. Surely, she never spoke? It was Starched Pat, her red hair pulled up into a tight bun on the top of her head. "How long have you been there?"

"What are you talking about? You've been laid there rambling away at me all morning. God knows what they put in those pills." She got up and took a step towards my wife, keeping her back to the bed in an effort to stop me hearing what they were saying about me.

"I thought he was better. Is he well enough to come home?"

"Better does not mean 'fully recovered'. He is calmer, certainly. He hasn't picked a fight with anyone for a while. He behaves himself in group therapy. But we're still rather concerned about the delusions and the paranoia. We think they can be kept under control with drugs, but they will suppress his mood. There will be less highs and lows, more of a flat-line."

"That sounds awful. I thought I was going to get my husband back."

"You have to realise that he is a paranoid schizophrenic. It is a long-term illness. We can't just make him better and send him home. The best we can do is to keep him under observation for a bit longer, keep it under control and be prepared for the odd relapse."

"But the banter's still there. He sounds pretty cheerful."

"We have noticed this. It's his way of dealing with the world around him. Inside, he probably feels lost and scared, surrounded by a society he does not trust and cannot relate to, but he has built a persona around him that masks his insecurity."

"And I fell in love with the mask?" Nurse Pat placed a comforting arm on hers. "Has he asked for anyone else - other visitors?"

"No."

"Anyone called Daphne?"

"Not on my watch."

"I'm still here, you know. I can hear every word." My little jenny wren, God bless her, sat on the bed, put her arms around me and held me tight.

"You're coming home with me, just as soon as they'll let me take you. We're going to be OK. We're going to be so OK."

We kissed briefly, then kissed again. Words no longer necessary. Long and deep, like we hadn't kissed in 10 years. My eyes closed and I sunk back into a deep and blissful sleep.

10th March 2018

"Why are we here?"

DI Baldwin lifted his left foot and inspected the evidence he'd picked up on the bottom of it. "A very good bloody question," he said, scraping it off on a thick clump of grass. "Christ that smells."

"Fox." Baldwin frowned at the unfeasibly childlike PCSO. "Country boy, me."

"Well, that explains one thing," said Baldwin.

"My Hampshire accent?"

"Boy or girl. It had been bothering me. We're not allowed to ask these days."

"I'm in a transitional stage."

"It's OK, Sam, I don't need any details. We're here to absorb the ambience of the scene of crime. The body was found where they've been excavating this copse. You're going to have to use your imagination, but where we're standing was once a house – a big old Victorian house."

"You could have fooled me."

"The house was boarded up when the site became a hospital, maybe even earlier. Unfit for habitation, I guess. Anyhow, nature claimed it back. The wildlife moved in and the place slowly collapsed 'til there was nothing much to see but a few crumbling walls among the rhododendrons and the brambles. But in the winter of '67, it seems, someone found their way into what was left of the cellar and got himself dead."

"So, they'd have to know it was here. Not the kind of thing you stumble over by accident. You can't see it from the road."

"Yes, my thoughts were running in that direction."

"1967 was a long time ago. There would have been more house and less copse, I suppose, back then."

"I suppose so. You'd have overlooked it from up there. You'd get a pretty good view from that end window."

"Maybe we could get some floor plans from that time. See whose office it was."

"I like your thinking, Sam. You'll go far. I did that yesterday. That floor was the maternity wing. The end room was used as a waiting room. Of course, absolutely anyone who worked here would have known about it. Not just doctors and nurses. Gardeners, window-cleaners, contractors...."

"So, what are we looking for down here? Surely forensics have been over the place."

"Humour me, Samuel."

"Samantha."

"Humour me, Samantha. You're lucky. I was thinking of coming at midnight."

"It's true what they say about you, isn't it? You're a bit weird."

14th August 1967

My eyes closed and I sunk back into peaceful slumber. She'd left me soon after that – to meet him outside. He was waiting for her in the car park. They kissed. I know they did. I woke in my armchair. My armchair, not the high-backed one at the mental hospital, or the stuffed horsehair in the maternity waiting room. This was our smart, new gold velour, 3-piece suite that we'd ordered as a coming-home treat. The one we could look forward to paying the HP on for the next 5 years.

"Where am I?" I called out, more for the joy of hearing the answer than for any other reason. My dutiful wife scampered in from the kitchen, a tea towel elegantly draped over one shoulder, flour coating her hands and apron.

"Don't worry, darling. I'm here. You had a nice sleep. Do you want some coffee – sorry, tea."

"I'd love some coffee."

"Yes, well you're not allowed. You know that. No stimulants. Weak tea or an orange juice. Which would you like?"

"Beer."

"Weak tea or orange juice."

"A tot of rum?" She turned back towards the kitchen. "A large one!"

"Weak tea, it is then," she called out, disappearing from view.

I stared out vacantly at life, what there was of it, going past. I'd been getting really good at that - plenty of practice. I looked for a beaten up old taxi. One that might whisk me off somewhere exotic – Timothy Whites perhaps, or the sweet shop. I could take a stroll by the river. I decided that I couldn't be bothered. Not yet.

13th March 2018

Ed Sheeran blared out unnecessarily loud. "Your phone!"

"Answer it, could you, my hands are wet!"

"It's some girl saying she's in love with your body!"

"That's the ringtone, Dad. Just swipe it."

"Swipe it? What, you mean nick it?"

"Give it here."

"It's stopped."

"Well, surprise, surprise. Look, if it rings again, you just swipe it, like this."

"Son, if I was born to be a secretary, I'd give it a try, but as I'm just a lazy old fart who thinks other people should get off their fat arses and answer their own phones, then I won't."

"Hello? Did you call me just now?.......Yes, that's me.......Baldwin?.......Yes, I remember – of course.......Why?.......Well, it's not that con -............Yes, yes, OK..........I'll ask him, but I don't think he'd want to - ....Oh - I suppose if you put it like that.........It's just – well, last time I only thought I'd be there a few minutes and you kept me filing in forms for over 3 hours.......Yes, yes, police work – I see.......I'll do my best........When you say, you'll send a car round, that's in a good way, isn't it?"

"Well?"

"That was Detective Inspector Baldwin. He's the bloke I spoke to last week. He wants me to go in again and review my statement."

"Review it? What, give it marks out of 10 like?"

"He wants to go over some of the details in more - detail."

"Likes his details, does he? Wants to leave no turn unstoned?"

"What he'd really like, actually, is to talk to you."

"Would he now?"

"He said he'd very much appreciate it if you'd come in to help them with their enquiries."

"Did he?"

"And it would be much better if you came in voluntarily."

15th November 1967

"Not yet. It's too early"

"What do you mean, it's too early? I've been sitting here for 3 months, staring out of this bloody window, twiddling my wotsits. It's doing me in. I was in the loony bin for 6 months before that. The last time I breathed fresh air was last February. It's November. I've forgotten what it smells like."

"Please don't call it that."

"What?"

"Loony bin. It sounds horrid."

"It was horrid. If you'd taken me to court and I'd got put away for thumping you – which I still don't believe I did, by the way, I'd have been out in less than 3 months. But no, you had me locked up in the loony bin, and now I'm confined to quarters."

"That's not fair. I didn't have you locked up. It was thanks to Dr. Sharp that you got proper treatment. You should be thankful. The police were all for stuffing you in a cell and throwing away the key."

"Oh yeah, let's all bow down to Dr. Sharp why don't we? That bloody man is the bane of my life. He's the wife beater, not me! Why doesn't he ever come here to see me, eh? He's supposed to be my doctor now. Why doesn't he visit one of his sick patients who's not allowed out of the house? Because he's ashamed, that's why. He knows what he's done to me, to us, to you!"

"You're getting yourself worked up again. You really need to calm down."

"I'm perfectly fucking calm!"

The boy started crying in the back room. It wasn't the first harsh words he'd ever heard, and I didn't suppose it would be the last. Did I really say those things to her, to the girl I loved so much? What had become of me? Where was my old lady in the red bonnet? Why couldn't she whisk me away from all this. Had I been abandoned even by her, to sit out the rest of my life in this chair, staring at a world I no longer felt a part of? Where was Daphne? Did she need me? Did she even remember me?

"Here, take this." My little jenny wren was holding out a small glass of water in one hand, a tiny yellow pill in the palm of the other.

"Ah, the little yellow peril. Have I been naughty again?"

"These are the ones that make you feel better, remember?"

"They put me to sleep. You like that though, don't you? You can go off and meet up with your fancy man while I'm off in the land of nod. Or does he come round here? Ah yes, maybe that's when he checks me over. He kills two birds with one stone." I swallowed the pill and closed my eyes, welcoming the haze that would soon envelope me.

"You'll feel better tomorrow," she said. I wanted her to know that I felt the warmth of the tear that landed on the back of my hand, but I couldn't find the words.

15th *March 2018*

"You need a bigger cubicle," said Sam, clutching a tray of four coffees and looking vainly for somewhere to put it.

"We'll use one of the interview rooms." DI Baldwin pushed his chair back as far as the partition would allow, but as this was only a few inches, having pulled his desk back to fit everyone in, this left him no room to stand and he was left, half crouched over his desk until his guests shuffled out of the cubicle in single file, and he could push his desk forward and himself upright. He straightened his tie and smoothed out the creases in his trousers with as much dignity as he could muster. "Took me 20 years to rise to a level where I didn't have to hot desk. Worth every minute, wasn't it?"

Fifteen minutes later, bearing a key purloined from the desk sergeant with no more effort than was needed to dig out of Sing Sing with a plastic spoon, and clutching four cups of cold coffee, they trooped into the interview room and arranged themselves around the table.

This was exactly the arrangement DI Baldwin had wanted to avoid. He had planned on something less intimidating. "Thank you for taking the trouble to come in, both of you. I'm hoping that you can fill me in on a few details."

"So I was told. What kind of details do you think I'd have that would be of the least use or interest 50 years after the event?"

"That's a very good question."

"I've got a million of them."

"Your son has provided us with some circumstantial evidence that your father might be the person that was discovered last Christmas on the Workhouse Fields Development."

"Yes, I know that."

"I understand you're not very happy that your son came to see us. In fact, you actively encouraged him not to."

"So?"

"I find that quite interesting."

"I'm glad you found it entertaining. I can juggle too, but please don't ask me to sing."

"It's funny, but it's often the people who don't want to talk to us who I most want to talk to."

"We all have our perverse pleasures"

"Dad. Sorry, Inspector but can I say something?"

"Haven't you said enough already?"

DI Baldwin spread both hands on the table, stretched his arms and took a deep breath. "Let's start again, shall we? I think we've stepped off on the wrong foot. This is just a friendly, informal chat. I want to identify a man who apparently died 50 years ago, and I think you can help me. If he does turn out to be your father, your grandfather, then I'd have thought you would be pleased you could put him to rest with some dignity – put a line under the matter and move forward with your lives." There was no response. "Let me ask you a few simple questions and see where it takes us."

"OK, Dad? You go ahead, Inspector, we wouldn't have come in at all if we weren't happy to co-operate."

"Your father – disappeared - when you were very young."

"Two or three."

"Two. If it was Christmas 1967, you were two, Dad."

"Thank you, but I'm interested to hear your father's opinion and then *I'll* do the deducting. I kind of get paid to do that bit and it's a lot less confusing if I do it on my own."

"Yeah, that's my thoughts exactly. You see, we do agree on some things, Inspector."

"What do you remember about him?"

"Nothing."

"That's not very helpful."

"That's what I thought. Done? We'll go now. There's no more to be said."

"Sit down! I'm sorry, I didn't mean to sound quite so startling. Please - sit down. I have some more questions."

"I've told you, I don't know anything. How is asking more questions going to get you anywhere?"

"Humour me. You may have been too young to know him personally, but I'm confident you will have learnt something about him from your mother, other relatives, friends of the family. Let's see if we can tease out anything useful."

"Tease away."

"What sort of a man was he?"

"What do you mean?"

"A family man? A workaholic? An alcoholic? A religious kind of a person? Was he good with children? Did he like animals? Anything at all that comes to mind."

"He might have been religious. Mum and Dad both sung in the church choir, I think. He was in the navy in the war. They both were, so they shared some memories of that together. Mum always called the floor the deck, and when she went into the kitchen, she called it the galley. I think they used talk to each other like that a lot. I suppose the war made a big impression on everyone in that generation."

"Your son tells me your father had an accident at sea."

"He dropped a shell on his foot."

"There you are, you see. You know lots about him. It *was* an accident was it?"

"What do you mean?"

"Lots of 'accidents' in wartime were self-inflicted. It was a way of getting away from the war zone, even if only for a while. People can do some desperate things when they're under stress."

"You saying he was a coward? He volunteered for the Royal Navy and he was proud to serve his country. He didn't hang around waiting for his call-up papers!"

"So, who told you that? It seems to me you know more about your father than you want to let on. Why is that, I wonder? Is there something about him you don't want me to know?" Baldwin waited for an answer, but none came. He looked at the grandson, but he too had gone uncharacteristically quiet. "Your silence is quite revealing. Perhaps we should play a game of 20 questions. Just yes or no answers, if that's easier for you. Did he have any strange fetishes?"

"What the hell - ?"

"Dressing up in ladies' clothes, perhaps. Being seen in the company of other men in secluded places?"

"I don't know what the hell game you think you're playing.....?"

"I'm trying to conduct an investigation. I'm trying to piece together possible scenarios based on the scanty evidence that I have in front of me. I'm trying to determine whether or not a serious crime has been committed and, if so, by whom, on who. And you are not helping me, and I don't know why, and I find that slightly disturbing."

24th December 1967

It was one of those crisp, winter days, when the sun tilts in low and bright with a cold, bloodless light. A nice day for a walk. She wasn't around for once. Last minute Christmas shopping, I expect. We'd had a quiet, birthday celebration lunch at home and I'd been allowed the luxury of half a glass of cheap white wine. I'd woken to the hollow sound of an empty house and, for once, no-one could stop me getting away from it. I settled on a brisk walk into town to stretch my legs and clear a few cobwebs. Maybe I could stop by the church, see if Daphne was around. She'd have forgotten what I look like. I found my shoes, neatly polished, and my best hat, clean and brushed, in their usual places, but I had to hunt for my coat. It wasn't hanging on a hook in the hall but had been tidily stowed away on a hanger in the wardrobe. Something weighed heavy in one of the pockets. It was my old clasp knife. Navy issue. Just a simple 4″ blade, like most penknives, but with the added bonus of a metal spike at the other end for getting boy scouts out of horses' hooves. I'd used it mainly for scraping out the bowl of my pipe in those long-lost, heady days when I was allowed to smoke. I left it there. I like those links with the past.

I was almost out of the door before it occurred to me that I didn't know if I would get back before she did. I hurriedly scribbled a note and wedged it under the corner of the (hideous) fruit bowl that had come from her (hideous) mother. Why hadn't she thrown that at me?! *Back soon. Gone for coffee! XXX*

The world had changed. There was something called *The Good, The Bad and The Ugly* playing at the Odeon. Another one of those weird, cheap westerns that looked like they were thrown together by school kids. Where was John Wayne when you needed him? As I passed the florist, a car drove by, too fast, it's windows wound down in spite of the bitter weather, kids laughing and joking inside, a radio or something blaring out. Those American kids off the telly, I think, singing about a daydream believer. I don't mind them having fun, but why do they assume we all want to join in? Bloody song. Once it's in your head, you can't get it out.

It took me 15 minutes to reach the church. I used to do it in less than 10, but nearly a year of forced idleness and a few too many pies had taken their toll. I had to stop to catch my breath twice. This was what I needed though, fresh air and exercise. This would do me a damn sight more good than pills and solitude. What did those bloody doctors know? The door still creaked reassuringly. Maybe I'd bring a can of 3-in-1 next time – or would I miss that sound?

I could hardly believe it. There she was, just sitting there, in our favourite pew. She smiled a welcome when I sat next to her, looking more beautiful than ever, golden hair tumbling to her shoulders, bright eyes flashing. "Welcome home," she said. "I've missed you."

"Sorry, I've been a bit down in the dumps lately. I haven't got out much."

"I know," she said. "You don't have to explain. I'm always here for you. I've been praying for you."

"Really?"

"Of course. And now you're here. It must have worked."

"Thank you." I felt a little tongue-tied.

"Don't leave me so long again, will you? I've been lonely without you."

"Daphne, are you happy at home?"

"I'm happy here, with you. That's all that matters. Let's just sit for a while."

We sat – communed maybe. We didn't really need words. Sometime later – I couldn't tell you how long – she squeezed my hand, got up, gathered her mop and bucket and disappeared through the vestry door. I thought I could see a bruise on the back of her leg. Or was it a just a dirty mark, or maybe a birthmark? I couldn't remember seeing it before. I left the church and wandered down the High Street. The bruise troubled me, but I felt calmer than I had felt for a long time, like a weight had been lifted, like I was seeing the world with more clarity. It seemed brighter and cleaner today.

Timothy Whites had gone. I'd turned my back for five minutes and someone had stolen it. In its place stood a gleaming, new branch of Marks and Spencer. A large poster in the window enticed people to step in and sample its new Food Hall. Always a sucker for a tempting offer, I stepped in. I could see now why there were so few people in the High Street, despite it being Christmas Eve. They were all in here. Bodies heaved to and fro. Large, sweaty mothers and small, fractious children argued, pulled and pushed in all directions. I was about to turn and flee when I remembered the driving force that had led me into town – the desire to purchase a small jar of very strong, instant coffee that could be secreted somewhere in the house and called upon in emergencies as medicinal back-up. I toyed with the idea, too, of a half-bottle of Navy Rum, but decided that discretion was the better part of valour.

As quickly as the crowd permitted, I grabbed the first jar that looked a likely candidate, paid for it and made my escape. I was back on the street before something struck my conscience with the full force of Henry's Hammer. It was Christmas Eve and I hadn't even thought about a present for her. That was probably why she left the house without telling me. She'd gone out to buy me a gift and was hoping to smuggle it indoors before I woke up. Christ, I was such a shitty husband. I wasn't about to turn around and tackle M & S again though. Not yet, at least. It would have to wait until the crowds subsided or I could find a less popular shop. I wandered further down the hill and found myself staring into the window of the bakery with a sudden determination to buy something to accompany the coffee - a large Danish pastry or something stuffed with cream.

The baker's heaved gently with like-minded shoppers. It was one of the old-fashioned variety, with a tall wooden rack in the middle of the store selling yesterday's sausage rolls and pasties at half-price. I queued dutifully. Three large women were picking over the pallid remains, comparing their finds and their common ailments with so little pause for breath that it was impossible to tell what was going soggy and what might have strange spots on it. I stood behind two small children discussing, with the intensity that only 6-year olds can achieve, the relative merits of macaroons and those things that look like ice-cream cornets but are actually made of marshmallow. Someone was ordering a spelt and honey loaf and giving detailed instructions about how it should be sliced; half thick and half thin slices, some for sandwiches and some for toasting.

And then I saw him, and something snapped. I have heard that a man in anger sees red. He just stood there, smiling at me. That smug, supercilious, wife-beating, wife-stealing, life-stealing smile and I saw nothing but red. I was going to wipe it from his face if it was the last thing I ever did. I tried to take a step towards him, to take his face and smash it into the glass counter, to hit him in the face and hit him again, and again until that smile was gone for good. But the pain that hit my chest squeezed all the life out me. My chest was suddenly caught between two demolition balls, crushing me front and back, the pain ripping through. Oblivion was my body's only form of defence.

They say that when a man dies, his life flashes before his eyes. My flashes lasted an eternity. I relived every moment as though for the first time, the fears, the smells, the pains, the laughter, the tears, all tumbled one upon each other in a kaleidoscope of memory. My fatherless childhood, the day I ran away to sea in search of adventure, attempts to run home for peace and safety, my marriage, my children, my poor dead children, my incarceration, my loneliness, my hate.

I gasped in a great bucket of air, my lungs straining with effort and pain. The crushing balls were now a pounding, bone-crushing beast, trampling me like an angry bull. It stopped suddenly and I choked in another great gobbet of air, wheezing and spluttering back to life. I lay there, panting for a few moments, no longer sure if I was in this world or the next.

"He's going to be OK. Has somebody called an ambulance? You just lay there and rest." Strong hands pressed my shoulders to the floor. "You're going nowhere just yet."

"Where am I?" I squeezed out.

"You are on the floor of the bakery. You've had a little heart attack, I do believe, but you're OK now. We need to get you to hospital as soon as we can and get you checked over. You're lucky I was here."

I opened my eyes, but I knew what I was going to see.

"Hello," he said "It's me, Paul – Dr. Sharp. You're supposed to be at home, aren't you? I told your wife that you shouldn't be getting up and about for another few weeks at least. You certainly shouldn't be wandering around on you own. I know you don't like to follow any of my advice, but I say these things for your own good. And here's why."

"Fuck off," I croaked, but it was ignored. He just threw that bloody awful smile back at me.

"What are we going to do with you?"

"Leave me alone!" I shouted, and lashed out with as much venom as I could muster. Spindly string-bean that he is, he shot backwards, his legs splaying out in all directions, the contents of his black bag scattering to every corner of the shop. I leapt to my feet and headed for the door. Three shocked, overweight and unprepared women proved no match for my shoulder charge and the momentum of my anger. I turned right out of the shop and, staggering like a drunk, headed down the hill towards the river. I needed to get away from all these people, to get some air back in my lungs - recover myself. My chest ached but the pain was nothing like the first searing agony. It took only minutes to cross the bridge and find the steps down to the tow path. There were benches along there. I could get my breath back. I should be undisturbed. I could get a bus back home in a few minutes. Maybe Sharp was right. I'd been an idiot to leave the house today but, yet again, it was *his* fault I was now in this state. I closed my eyes and fought off a growing feeling of nausea.

"Hey!"

"There he is!"

"He's still alive!"

People were standing on the bridge, waving and pointing – interfering little bastards. I could see Dr. Sharp, head and shoulders above the others, crossing the bridge behind them and then making his way down the steps and heading towards me. I could have tried to run. I wanted to, but I knew that it was pointless. He was younger and fitter. I would keel over and die in the attempt. Anyway, what was this useless little fart going to do to me? I expected him to be angry, to want revenge for his humiliation, to offer endless lies and excuses. He sat beside me and said nothing at first. He looked at me as though I were a naughty schoolboy.

"I do understand." he said in a pathetic attempt at sympathy. "I think I know how you feel. You've had a shock. We'll just take things at your pace. OK? No pressure. I do think you should go to the hospital. There can be complications after a heart attack. They can do a few simple tests – find out just how bad it was – if there's any lasting damage. Most of all, you need rest. In a few days you'll be ready to take some exercise. Perhaps we could start with a gentle walk to the end of the road, eh – instead of jumping straight into a boxing match. That's a decent uppercut you've got there. You could give Henry Cooper a run for his money."

"Come anywhere near my wife once more and you'll feel it again."

"We've talked about this before, haven't we? I know you find it hard to accept, but there is nothing, and there never has been anything, between me and your wife. We have never met outside of a purely professional – "

I got up and walked away – further along the tow path. I wasn't going to listen to his feeble lies. And I wasn't going to face the interfering busy bodies who were still staring and pointing from the bridge, laughing behind my back at the useless cuckold and his arrogant Incubus. He scampered along behind me.

"Get away from me!"

"I can't leave you like this. You're not well. Please, come back here. I'll come to the hospital with you."

"Fuck off!" I quickened my pace, although how I thought I would shake off this irritating limpet God only knows. In 100 yards or so there was a gap in the bank to my left. Unkempt hedges had overgrown an old passageway, but a few crumbling steps led upwards – a possible escape route. I ducked into it, scratching my face and hands on thick stems of brambles, their thorns guarding the entrance against unwary travellers. I tried to take the steps two at a time, but the pain that shot across my chest soon put paid to that. The steps quickly petered out into an ancient stony path, greasy with clumps of damp grass, weeds and puddles of glutinous mud. I could hear him somewhere, still behind me, calling out my name, calling me to stop, swearing at the overgrown hedgerows. A flash of red to my right revealed a narrow gap in a row of rotting fence panels. I squeezed through and found myself in a muddy slick of browned leaves under a canopy of silver birches and beech trees. The ground still sloped upwards. Beyond the stand of trees was a band of gorse and more densely packed brambles with ancient rhododendrons thrusting through them, and beyond them, an imposing red-brick, Victorian building, which, even from this unusual angle, could be nothing else but the back of the recently vacated hospital.

He was still there, somewhere behind the rotting fence, shouting now, panicking, cursing.

The copse of rhododendrons offered a possible hiding place. I could be secure there for a while. No-one would find me. He would soon give up the chase. I slipped and scrambled my way up the hill, grabbing at low hanging branches of beech to pull myself up. A deep pool of sticky mud and rotting leaves sucked at my left foot, eager to hold me back. My shoe disappeared into the quagmire and I was left to continue without its protection from the twigs and sharp leaves that threw themselves in my way. I leaned against a sturdy birch tree, panting hard, regretting the whim that had drawn me from the house today. I looked for a gap in the gorse and brambles that might lead me to a hiding place and there, standing no more than 10 feet in front of me, was my little old lady, wrapped in her thick winter cape, her red bonnet firmly knotted under her chin. A bony hand emerged from the cape and beckoned me in. She smiled her reassuring smile and I followed, confident that she would keep me safe.

She was standing in the shadow of a crumbling wall of red brick that matched the empty buildings beyond. I could see more broken stretches of walls and what was left of a few rotted window and door frames. Ivy and brambles had broken their way through them, and tall rhododendrons had undermined the footings, but it was clear that once a building had stood here. I remembered now. I had seen this many times while standing in the waiting room, smoking endless cigarettes or sucking nervously on my pipe. Children called it the witch's house. I could vaguely recall tales of ghostly sightings, but the details had never interested me.

Another shout behind me, and the splintering of a fence, jolted me back to life. I took a step or two towards the beckoning woman, trying vainly to avoid stones and sharp holly leaves. What looked like part of a wooden floor, or a pine door that had fallen over, lay in my way. I stepped on it. It seemed the easiest path. But the wood was rotten, nothing but a veneer of safety, a trick left in my path. I crashed through and tumbled down into some kind of underground cavern, a black hole that swallowed me into unconsciousness.

I came to with Sharp slapping me round the face. "Wake up, man!" he was shouting. "We have to get you out of here!" I was groggy and the pain across my chest made breathing difficult, but I was aware enough to know that I did not like being slapped.

I pushed him away. "Get off me!" He fell backwards, landing on his backside in a puddle of murky water. A dim light filtered through the hole above us. A blackened slope led to the world outside. Too high and steep for one man to clamber up very easily, but the two of us together should manage it. Not yet though. I laid there, my back propped against the dank, stone wall, dazed and breathing heavily. Sharp sat in his puddle, staring malevolently.

"Well, this wasn't quite what I was expecting from a typical day at work when I took the Hippocratic oath." Smooth bastard. Always had some smartass comment to make. "How are you feeling?" he continued. "Do you have any pain in the chest?"

"Yes – and one in the arse."

"I'm trying to help you. A little gratitude wouldn't go amiss."

"For what? For not reporting you to the Medical Board for gross misconduct? For letting you fuck my wife when my back is turned. For giving us a son?"

"Did you take your tablets this morning? We did warn you that there could be relapses but there is normally a trigger of some kind."

"There's nothing wrong with me. It's you. You've been hounding me for years. Do you think I'm stupid? I can see what's going on."

"There is nothing 'going on' except what's going on inside your head. Paranoid schizophrenia is a very complex disorder. You are subject to delusions, depression, feelings of inadequacy and of persecution. I understand that some of your anger and frustration is directed at me. It is often directed at the ones we love and at those in authority. But believe me, I have nothing but your best interests at heart, as I do for all my patients. Your wife loves you dearly and has stood by you for the last two years with nothing but devotion and endless patience. You are an incredibly lucky man. I have known many cases, often less severe than yours, who have been permanently sectioned because they do not have the love and care of a family behind them. Embrace that care. Go home, take your medicines, look after yourself. You might never be fully free from your disorder, but it need not ruin your life. Don't let it ruin the lives of the people around you."

We sat in silence for a few seconds, shivering in the damp and the cold.

"Why do you do it?" I asked. I was calmer now. My chest throbbed but it felt less tight. Breathing was a little easier.

"I always wanted to be a doctor. I could never imagine doing anything else. My grandfather was a surgeon. My mother was a nurse. It just seemed natural."

"That's not what I meant. Why do you beat her?"

"I don't beat anybody."

"Your wife, Daphne, she's told me. I've seen the bruises. There is no point in lying about it."

We sat there in silence with only the regular, slow drip of water leaking into the cellar somewhere in the darkness to measure time. He broke the silence first.

"What does your God say to you?"

"What makes you think He talks to me?"

"I know you go to church a lot. Your wife has told me that you go almost every week, to pray. You sometimes spend hours there. The vicar has seen you many times. You have your favourite pew where you sit in contemplation. He says he hears you muttering your prayers. That must give you great comfort. I sometimes wished that I had grown up with a faith like that, but ours was a scientific household. They were atheists, my parents. They had no time for Christianity, well, for any religion."

"I've seen the bruises. You can't deny it."

"I don't beat my wi – " He stopped mid-sentence – giving himself thinking time to piece together his next lie. That's the trouble with liars. They're constantly having to remember their lies and excuses. Constantly living in fear their lies will catch them out. "I don't *have* a wife," he said. "I don't know who Daphne is, but she is not my wife. I have never had a wife. I will never have a wife."

"You must think I was born yesterday. I'm not an idiot you know."

"Believe me. I have no interest in women." He waited a few seconds and tried a different tack. It was obvious he was trying to catch me out. "Tell me about Daphne. Do you confide in her? Where do you meet? What makes you think we are married?"

"Shut up!"

"Your wife is very worried. She is convinced you are having an affair with this woman."

"She knows nothing about Daphne. There is no affair. You won't drive a wedge between us like that! Our marriage is strong. You won't drive us apart!"

"And yet you feel the need to seek companionship elsewhere. Or do you? You wife tells me that you speak to Daphne in your sleep. You mentioned her name a couple of times in your sessions with von Rothschild. He said something very interesting to me."

"Really? He never said anything that interested me."

"He said that perhaps Daphne does not exist." He paused. "What do you feel about that?"

I exploded. "Don't say that! It's not true! You can't take *her* away from me as well, you bastard!" The pain welled up in my chest again. I clutched at my heart and called out in pain.

He leaned across quickly and grabbed at my tie. "You must try to calm down. Let me loosen your tie, undo your top button. You need to breath. Now - "

"Leave me alone!" I bellowed. "Get off me! I don't want your stinking hands all over me!" I barely knew what I was doing, but in those few brief seconds, I reached inside my coat pocket and, with a practiced thumb, flicked open the marlin spike on my clasp knife. I grabbed him by the throat with my left hand and, gripping the knife in the other, the spike wedged between my fingers, I thrust it upwards into his chest. Whether I was accurate enough or the spike was long enough to pierce his heart, I doubted, but his shock hissed out of him like a deflating football. I expected him to collapse on me, but the sudden shock and pain filled him with enormous strength. His hands had been gripping my tie, but he flung them apart, breaking my grip on his throat and sending the knife skittering across the cobbled floor. Before I knew it, his long bony fingers were locked around my throat, squeezing and shaking me. He was shouting obscenities at me, his own anger and frustration suddenly set free. I could not breath, I felt nausea welling up from deep inside, grappling in my chest with the throbbing pain that still enveloped me. I tried to prize his fingers from my throat, but they held firm in a deathly grip. I tried to land blows to his head and body but there was no room to swing my fists with enough force. I was feeling weak and ready to pass out. I managed to grasp his neck with both my hands. It was so scrawny, as though I might snap it like a chicken's.

We were locked together, both weakening, wrestling in the gloom, coal-dust kicking up plumes of acrid air, choking us even more. Somehow, I rolled on top of him. His head cracked down on the stone floor. I lifted it again and smacked it down with all my remaining strength. His hair turned blood-red, but his grip tightened even more, his body arching in a desperate effort to squeeze the life out of me. Dizziness and nausea swept over me. I tried to keep my grip, but I could feel it slipping. He was using his longer reach to lever me away. I tried to redouble my efforts, but I was fading fast.

"Kill me," she croaked out. "Kill me!" Her red bonnet almost smothered her face now, but I could see her eyes bulging with the delight of her imminent release, and her grimace of a smile as she sank back into welcome oblivion.

21st March 2018

There was a feeble tap on the partition in front of DI Baldwin. He looked up, then across at the clock on the wall. It was ten to eight.

"I'm not here."

"You will be when I show you this." It was the pre-pubescent tones of Samuel/Samantha. A hand appeared above the partition, waving a large brown, internal-mail envelope – the sort that large organisations once used for passing documents from one office to another before the chance discovery of internets and e-mail.

"I thought you said I was the weird one."

"I also come bearing coffee." Sam squeezed into the tiny cubicle with two mugs in one hand and the envelope in the other. "Good and strong with two lumps, just how you like your women."

"Something like that. I haven't seen you for a bit. Did they make you do some real work?"

"No, I'm still in Traffic. Just knocked off. They let me go 15 minutes early tonight for good conduct."

"So, you thought you'd spend it pestering me again. Don't you have a home to go to?"

"No." It sounded genuine. "I've solved your case for you."

"Oh good – which one?"

"The Workhouse Fields one. The dead body in the coal cellar. You took me there, remember?"

"That was when I thought you were a proper copper."

"You'll laugh on the other side when you see this." Sam slid the envelope across the desk.

"Your face – the other side of your face."

"Eh?"

"You're meant to say, 'the other side of your face' when you – never mind." He glanced down at the envelope. "This is addressed to me."

"Yes. It's from Archives."

"I'm honoured. They've never sent me presents before."

"You asked for it apparently."

"Did I? What is it"

"It's a missing persons' report, and it makes very interesting reading."

"You've read it?"

"Yes."

"It's addressed to me."

"Yes."

"When you say that you've solved my case, do you mean that you've opened my mail and read the private and confidential information stored therein? The private and confidential information Inside the envelope addressed to me and clearly marked 'private and confidential'?"

"Yes."

"You'll go far. We'll make a detective of you yet. Save me the bother of reading it for myself and tell me all about it."

"You asked Archives to look out any missing persons' reports, or anything odd, they said, from around Christmas 1967. Apparently, they've had this down there for 3 weeks waiting for you to pick it up."

"The phone system hasn't reached as far as the basement yet then?"

"Apparently not." Sam just sat there, looking smug.

"Any minute now you're going to tell me what's in the envelope."

"Oh yes, sorry. So, on 28th December 1967 someone called Edward Willis (liked to be called Ted) reported a missing person – a certain Paul Sharp – a doctor no less."

"Not our guy then. And who was Ted Willis?"

" He put his relationship down as 'friend' but then crossed it out and put 'flatmate'. He shared the same address as the mis-per."

"Miss Per? Who - ?"

"Mis-per – missing person – they use it on all the police programmes."

"I never watch them."

"Anyway, this doctor leaves his surgery on the afternoon of 24th December 1967 but doesn't make it home."

"But the boyfriend doesn't report it until after Christmas?"

"Boyfriend?"

"Ted Willis."

"You worked that out quick."

"Experience."

"They'd had words apparently, before the doctor left for work. Ted thought his 'flatmate' had decided to visit his Aunt over Christmas because of the argument, but when he didn't turn up for surgery on 27th December, and still didn't get home that night then he thought he'd better report it."

"And he was never found?"

"Ah, now that's where it gets interesting. He wasn't found because he was never missing."

"I'm regretting ever letting you get involved with this."

"That's why this missing persons' report never made it on to HOLMES. It was a dead case. Nothing to report."

"Lucky someone held on to it then."

"This is Archives we're talking about. They're professional hoarders. On 2nd January 1968, some vagrant calling himself Dr. Sharp walked into Bournemouth Police Station and said he'd seen on the news that he was meant to be missing and could they please call the search off because there he was."

"Did the Aunt live in Bournemouth?"

"No, Sheffield."

"And how do we know all this?"

"Bournemouth phoned us and someone at this end noted it on the missing persons' report. They must have thought the fact that the bloke looked like a tramp was interesting enough to put down on the report. However, the tramp was able to prove who he was - "

"How?"

"He produced a driving licence. "

"But nobody followed it up."

"Not as far as I can see. They'd contacted the Aunt through Yorkshire Constabulary, but he wasn't there. His car was at the garage being serviced but he hadn't collected it by then. Ted Willis made two calls to see if he'd been found. They told him he'd turned up in Bournemouth and they never heard from him again. Case closed."

"I'm lost. How have you solved anything?"

"I went on to HOLMES - see if I could find out anything about Paul Sharp – nothing."

"When did you do that?"

"This afternoon."

"So how long have you had this file?"

"Since this morning."

"And this is the kind of thing they let you do in Traffic, is it"

"I get breaks. Here's my theory. Sharp and Willis are lovers."

"I got that bit."

"They have a lovers' tiff. Willis tells the police they argued on the morning of 24th, but I'm guessing it was later, Christmas Day, or Boxing Day, perhaps. He kills Sharp and then hides the body in the cellar of that old building."

"Why?"

"So that no-one would find it."

"Mmm. Why there?"

"The clues are all here," said Sam, triumphantly slapping his hand down on the brown envelope. "He was a nurse!"

"Well, that clinches it."

"He knew about the cellar, because he worked at the hospital. He knew the site was abandoned and over the Christmas period, it couldn't have been too difficult to haul the body there, with nobody about."

"Hauled a lot of dead bodies about have you?"

"Then he leaves it a few days, goes to Bournemouth, pretends to be Dr. Sharp and announces himself alive and well."

"And why did he go dressed as a tramp?"

"Disguise. Two reasons. He didn't want to be recognised as Ted Willis, but he also needed to pass himself off as Paul Sharp. So, he doesn't shave for a week, adds some grease and grime, maybe embellishes his story with a tale about his car breaking down or something - I'm guessing now – "

"Don't."

"What?"

"Don't ever guess. You only work with facts. It's a nice story, but in the space of 5 minutes you've presented me with a dead man I've never heard of, killed by someone nobody knows."

"Ah, but we do know Ted Willis." Baldwin knitted his brow. "I looked him up on HOLMES too."

"Not a penny of the taxpayers' money is ever wasted on you, is it?"

"Ted Willis was known to be a homosexual."

"That's not illegal. In fact, it was decriminalized in 1967."

"But it was illegal in 1953. He was arrested at the age of 25 in a *compromising position,*" Sam's fingers indicated the speech marks, "in the gentlemen's lavatory at the train station."

"Which means that 14 years later he was bound to commit a murder."

"No, but perhaps it gives us an idea about their lifestyles."

"When's the next Olympics? I'm going to enter you for the high conclusions." Baldwin reached into the bottom draw of his desk and pulled out a large plastic wallet. He tipped the contents onto his desk and arranged them in neat rows, as he had many times before. "These are facts, Sam. Things we found with the body. We don't know if they belonged to the body or to someone else. For some things, we don't know if they were left at the scene before the dead body or after it or with it, but if we ever solve this conundrum, we will have to be sure that these facts fit that solution." He pulled open a thin pink file and spilled a few photographs on the desk. These he picked up one at a time and placed face up in another neat row facing Sam. "I don't believe you've seen these."

"Oh."

"This is the back of the skull."

"Ouch."

"Forensics tells us that the wounds didn't heal at all before he died. This happened immediately before death, and probably caused or contributed to the death. There would have been a lot of blood."

"I see why it's not just a 'missing person'."

"We never tell the press everything, Sam. We'd never catch anyone."

"Could he have just fallen in, hit his head, and died?"

"Nothing's impossible, except there's this." Baldwin picked up the remnants of a shoe from the small collection of evidence and placed it in front of Sam. "Size 7, black leather, good quality, what's left of it."

Sam picked up the shoe, turned it over, although he had no idea what he was looking for, sniffed it, "The kind of shoe a doctor would wear, I guess," and placed it back on the desk.

"Not this doctor, if that's what he was – size 7 – forensics tell us that, given the size of the bones in his feet, this guy took a size 10 at least, maybe 11."

"So, this would have been snug."

"And where's the other one?"

"Eaten by rats? Carried off?" Sam was looking less confident now. He could see his solidly thought through theory about to crumble under Detective Inspector Baldwin's meticulous analysis.

"Maybe, but if it was rats, they would have left something surely, even if it was only the metal eyelets or the nails in the heel. And what animal would have carried off a shoe but left the body intact? The bones weren't disturbed until the day he was found. So – "

"So, there were two people – "

"At least."

"So, there were at least two people. One of them, possibly the killer, left with the victim's shoes and left one of his behind. What else have we got?"

"We?"

"Yes – we."

Baldwin smiled. "I want you to take a look at this photo."

Sam studied the grainy, monochrome image of a skeleton propped up against a blackened wall. The white skeleton stood out starkly against the dark background, making it look like a painted image. "He's sitting up, leaning against a wall. There's some kind of metal grill behind him and that's leaning against a sloping wall."

"It's a coal chute. That's where they got in."

"And out?"

"Definitely. Look closer."

Sam picked up the photograph and held it closer. "His arms are hooked over that metal grill."

"Very good. The grill is holding him slightly away from the wall and the coal dust has not been disturbed immediately behind him. He's far enough away from the wall that you can be confident he was placed there after he sustained the head injury - either after he was dead, or he died in that position."

"Why would the killer do that?"

"Because the only way out was through the coal hole above them, but it was too high for a man to reach. He needed something to stand on."

"Yes, that works," said Sam, putting down the photo and reaching for coffee.

"You missed something." Baldwin picked up a pen and pointed at the same photograph. The pen hovered over the skeleton's head.

Sam leant over the desk. "I don't – oh, what's that?"

"It's a hat - a bonnet to be precise."

"It's tied round his neck."

"Apart from the shoe and a leather belt, there wasn't much left in the way of clothing. Just the remains of a coat that had probably been thrown over the body. We retrieved the jar of coffee, three shillings and seven pence ha'penny in coins and this old pocket watch from it, but what was left of the coat disintegrated. It was very damp down there. All the rest of the clothing had rotted away over the years."

Sam picked up the photo again and stared at it for a few moments. "But this bonnet seems to be intact."

"Yes. Any thoughts?"

"Somebody added it later?"

"Maybe."

"Where is it now? You've got all this other stuff here but there's no bonnet."

"It never got bagged. Forensics swear blind there *was* no bonnet when they were sweeping the place. I spoke to the photographer. He says he doesn't remember seeing it."

"But it's there in the photo."

"Yes. Strange, don't you think? Another part of the mystery – another fact we need to slot into its proper place." Baldwin's pen moved to the last photo in the row. "I still think it's this guy."

"Is this Grandad?"

"Yes."

"Funny looking little guy, isn't he? He looks a bit like Norman Wisdom."

Baldwin looked at Sam, and Sam looked back. Their minds, for once perhaps, in tune. "I wouldn't be surprised if Grandad wore size 7 shoes," said Baldwin.

Sam reached for the brown envelope, slid out the yellowed missing persons' report and ran his finger down the front page. "Six foot three. Paul Sharp was six foot three. Did they measure all the bones?"

"I don't know."

"Call them."

DI Baldwin glanced at the clock again - 8:30. "They won't be there. It can wait."

"Of course it can't wait. Get them out of bed if you have to. We need to know how tall this guy was!"

Baldwin picked up the old silver pocket watch and opened the case by clicking the crown with his thumb. "He sat there for 50 years, Sam, patiently waiting for someone to find him. Another night won't hurt." He placed the open watch in front of Sam and pointed at the message engraved inside the cover. *'To my favourite Grandson on his 21st - 24th Dec. 1938.'*

Sam sank back into the chair like a petulant child. "You've had that all this time."

"I have, but what I can't be certain of, is whether Grandad is the killer or the victim, or if there is another explanation why his belongings were there." DI Baldwin carefully placed all the evidence and photographs in the plastic wallet and locked it in his bottom draw. "Come on, son, the pubs are still open."

"I've never drunk beer."

"Do you believe in ghosts?"

"Of course not."

"Then I shall tell you a story about Charlie Snooks and his faithful wife Ethel. How they tortured and murdered unknown numbers of workhouse boys and girls; how Ethel was the procurer, but Charlie was the killer, and how their mortal bodies were never laid to rest in consecrated ground. I shall tell you how Ethel was murdered by Charlie and how Charlie engineered his own death and, as we ponder their wretched lives and deaths, we will muse on what might have happened to the boy who was born on the day they died; the boy who was saved from their clutches only to find his life entwined with theirs, and by the time I'm finished, you will be begging me for beer."

"I'm more of a Long, Slow, Comfortable Screw Up Against a Wall kind of a girl, actually."

Baldwin turned out the last of the office lights and they headed downstairs. For once, Baldwin couldn't think of a single thing to say.

THE END

Printed in Great Britain
by Amazon

23758334R00078